Belén López Peiró

WHY DID YOU COME BACK EVERY SUMMER

Translated by
Maureen Shaughnessy

CHARCO PRESS

'López Peiró narrates the experience of sexual abuse that she endured while she goes a young girl. But she doesn't do so in the first person. Rather, she does it through parallel voices and police statements which allow her to widen out a tragedy that in no case is singular. It is always plural.'
Paloma Abad, *VOGUE*

'*Why Did You Come Back Every Summer* marks an inflection point in the chronology of autobiographical fiction.'
Jorge Carrión, *The Washington Post*

'The map of what happens to us, finally revealed complete. Indispensable.' **Brigitte Vasallo**

'An exquisite book, a powerful political intervention.'
Gabriela Cabezón Cámara

'A perfect and precise book that tackles macho violence and makes the picture that supports impunity emotionally palpable.' **Gabriela Wiener**

'Employing direct and crude language, López Peiró writes against the system, against the web of silence that tried to keep her quiet, and against herself. (...) A book that becomes a political act that forces us to look in places we would prefer not to.' *Casa Amèrica Catalunya*

'Crude, direct and without embellishment, Peiró's novel has become a literary revolution that has put the wind in the sails of all the women who have been in her position.'
Cynthia Serna Box, *El independiente*

'One of the bravest and harshest texts in recent memory.'
Agustina Larrea, *Infobae*

WHY DID YOU COME BACK EVERY SUMMER

First published by Charco Press 2024
Charco Press Ltd., Office 59, 44-46 Morningside Road, Edinburgh
EH10 4BF

Work published with funding from the 'Sur' Translation Support
Programme of the Ministry of Foreign Affairs of Argentina / Obra
editada en el marco del Programa 'Sur' de Apoyo a las Traducciones del
Ministerio de Relaciones Exteriores de la República Argentina.

A CIP catalogue record for this book is available
from the British Library.

ISBN: 9781913867805
e-book: 9781913867812

www.charcopress.com

Edited by Fionn Petch
Cover designed by Pablo Font
Typeset by Laura Jones
Proofread by Fiona Mackintosh

FOREWORD

by
Gabriela Cabezón Cámara

In order to write, you have to write. The notion of inspiration catching hold of you as you're working is a cliché. You might think this means you only make gradual progress, like when you train for a sport. Today I ran 100 metres, next week I will run 110, and in a month, I will be running 300. But no. Writing doesn't happen like that. You have to write 110 for as long as all you can give is 110. It might be a month or a year. And then, at some point, no one knows how it happens. Suddenly you are running a thousand metres. All the tools that you've develop, the images you've tried to create, the fluidity of language, the singular music of a text. The thing you've been seeking for months, suddenly materialises. I call it 'the event'. It doesn't always happen.

It did happen to Belén. She felt the desire to write and, since she's someone who acts in accordance with her desires, she set to. She tried. She persevered. In one direction, then another, in a certain way, then another. She read a lot and she wrote some more. And one day, out of the blue, almost like a tsunami, the quantum leap: a new perspective (new perspectives), the rough voices, the harsh music. And at the heart, silence. Almost total silence. The event: Belén was writing a text that already had a power of its own. It had happened. Here it was. It had come to Belén: she'd given birth to her text. Her text was alive.

Belén had fought hard to make it happen. And it happened when her decision to write met with a public call for entries issued by the Grandmothers of the Plaza de Mayo organisation: to write about identity. From that friction between her own desire and an external proposal, fire was born. It burned fiercely. When Belén read those first few pages out loud, it was astonishing. Because of what she was telling, of course, but especially because of how she was telling it. How had she come up with the idea of telling her story from so many perspectives? How had she managed to light up that silence at the centre? From the beginning, the structure she was weaving together was palpable. And it was incredible.

There were more questions, certainly. Where was she taking her courage from, for instance. Because, to be able to speak up like that, you need the kind of courage you cannot build in a single day. The courage needed for this book has taken years, a lifetime. The courage to put herself through the questions, and then more questions, and the trials and perversions of the justice system – as well as its sheer slowness. It was this same courage that motivated her while she was writing this harsh and beautiful book. It happened while she was building this discovery, that first intuition, the very first representation of all the noise, of the voices that overwhelm – and also hush – whoever dares to speak up. It was as she was diving into this world that she managed to get out of it entirely. When she typed the last full stop, Belén was no longer a victim. She was a writer who'd written an incredible book and had left behind, in the past, an abuse. And also a great part of the pain that she'd endured. Through her writing, two births occurred: an author of consequence. And a strong woman.

I'm not sure if Belén ever suspected what was coming once the event had taken place. I don't think she could have done. *Why Did You Come Back Every Summer* was not just a success story in the literary world. It was a lot more than that. It ended up being woven into a great social struggle. A historical fight. This meant – means, still – a huge act of bravery. To be questioned time and again, and again and again, on the abuse she suffered when she was a teenager. And to have to answer. Each time. To put up with that demand. From the press and from the thousands, the millions of girls that have gone through something similar. To put up with – also – the fact that a lot less attention than she deserved was paid to the writer's craft: to literature, to form.

But dear reader, male or female: pay close attention. If this book grabs you and amazes you, it's because the formal work that was done here is extraordinary. While you are reading, have a close look. Ask yourself how she's managed to represent this hell. The hell of the voices belonging to others. The estranged discourse of the justice system, the inconsiderate, brainless opinions of so many. How did she do it? How did she imagine it? How did she manage to weave them all into a single music that gave them cohesion, rhythm, a soulful beat?

What you are about to read is the work of an author who was once a victim of horrific abuse. But make no mistake. She is no longer a victim. She is a strong woman who has decided that her life is about literature.

And she is a damn good writer.

So then, why did you come back every summer? Do you like to suffer? Why didn't you just stay home? There, in Buenos Aires, dying of heat. Ah. No. That's right – it's because you couldn't. You didn't have anyone to take care of you. Now it makes sense. We were the ones to help you, we gave you a family – and this is how you repay us? We didn't love you, we only invited you here because your mum showered us with gifts. She gave us dresses, paid for trips and perfumes. All in exchange for having you here. Taking you out to dinner with us, taking you out for a walk, like a dog. We taught you how to clean. You stopped being the helpless little city girl who didn't even know how to make her own bed. Or wash the dishes, you always left them dirty in the sink. Here we handed you the broom and you started to sweep. We gave you some rags and a can of furniture polish and you learned to shine. First the bedrooms, then the living room and the kitchen last. Always in that order. Do you remember? You even got mad once when we left your bag out on the patio so it wouldn't clutter up the house. Or when we threw out your tattered espadrilles and your hormone-stained underwear. Listen here, in this house we put up with everything except filth. So, naturally, your anger built up... but now you've taken it too far. To be honest, I wasn't expecting this. You've always been jealous of Florencia because she had lots of friends, because she could go out dancing and had many clothes. Oh but, wait. I know why you did it. Because she has a family who loves her. And you don't.

CRIMINAL COMPLAINT AFFIDAVIT

For the attention of the Court:

I.   SCOPE

I, the undersigned, hereby file an official complaint for the commission of a crime subject to public prosecution of which I was a victim, and therefore request the immediate intervention of justice to commence a criminal investigation in order to establish the facts and identify the perpetrators.

(Pursuant to article 149 bis and related provisions of the National Code of Criminal Procedure)

II.   DEFENDANT

Be it known to all persons that the individual herein described is a male party who is gainfully employed as a member of the Argentine Ministry of Security in the Province of Buenos Aires. He is forty-seven years old and currently holds the rank of police commissioner. He resides at 86 Calle Belgrano, Santa Lucía, Province of Buenos Aires.

III.   BACKGROUND

I hereby declare that I was born on 24 February 1992 in the city of Buenos Aires. My immediate family includes my mother, my father and one brother. I am presently twenty-two years old and am filing this statement to recount the experiences, hardships and suffering I endured during my adolescence. It is my earnest desire to seek justice for these events. My uncle sexually abused me repeatedly between the ages of thirteen and seventeen.

IV.   LEGAL DEFINITION
Pursuant to the foregoing declaration, and without prejudice to the possibility that this inquiry may lead to the discovery and identification of other culpable parties, the alleged behaviour described herein conforms to the definition for the offence of 'SEXUAL ABUSE' as specified in article 119 of the Argentine Criminal Code.

V.   PETITION
Given the foregoing, I hereby request:

1.   That charges be brought and a hearing convened for purposes of ratification.

2.   That a criminal investigation be commenced in order to ascertain the circumstances and identify the wrongdoers.

If the aforementioned petition is granted, justice shall be served.

He rang the buzzer and I let him in. I knew he'd show up sooner or later. He came by our apartment every time he travelled to La Plata, at least once a month. It was his pitstop. He came to refuel, to grease up his dick. Anticipating his next visit felt like a meat locker going rancid in the sun.

My mother had gone to work that morning. She almost always took the bus at noon, but that day the magazine offices were closing early and my brother was at work. So I was alone, lying in my single bed in my room with pink walls, wearing the summer pyjamas my godmother had given me for my fifteenth birthday: a pair of turquoise shorts that hung low on my hips and a black tank top printed with dancing butterflies on the chest.

He walked into the apartment with a smile on his face, still wearing his uniform. I had forgotten what it was like to have to untie his boots. He set his gun down on top of the dining room cabinet, up high where it was almost out of view, and went to my brother's room to get undressed. He wanted a quick shower before heading out on the road. I got back into bed and closed my eyes.

The pitter-patter of the water hitting the shower floor pierced through me. I pictured him naked, rinsing off with my soap. But no. Suddenly he opened the door to my room, shirtless, still in his faded yellow boxers. He asked if I wanted a massage. 'We can use your mum's gel', he said. I told him no, but he didn't listen. Before I knew it he was right behind me. He ripped back the sheets and lifted up my shirt. He pulled my shorts and underwear down to my knees.

The first shiver came when he rubbed that gel on my back. I froze. But then I turned my head to the side and looked at him. I saw his hard dick. With one hand he was touching my butt and with the other he was jerking off, slowly, in no rush to come. My only reaction was in fact my last hope: I pushed against the mattress and tried to get up but he pushed me back down with his free hand, and now I could no longer see, nor breathe. I could only feel the trembling of my lips and the crunching of my bones as he hefted his sickening 150-kilo body on top of me. I was suffocating.

The buzzer rang. There was someone at the door trying to get in. I'd accidentally left my keys in the lock. He got up and ran back to the shower. The water was still on and the noise of the buzzer became more insistent. I don't remember how, but I got back on my knees, pulled up my shorts and walked from my bed to the front door. I opened it. It was my dad, back home for lunch. I hugged him and told him I wanted to go back to sleep. For a moment I was reminded of what it was like not to be scared and who I had been before the danger closed in on me like a trap.

Everything started when he hurt you. Of course we know you weren't asking for it. It wasn't your fault, even though he made you feel otherwise. But he *touched* you. *He* was the one to touch *you*. What are you going to do about it? We all have our cross to bear. Yours turned out to be big and heavy, that's for sure, but it could always be worse. At least he didn't rape you. Or so you think. But when it comes down to it, you're the one who kept the pain coming. That's right. Because he started it. He really put you through the wringer. He manhandled you, knocked you down, trampled you. He dragged you all over kingdom come, left you out to dry, jammed his fingers inside you and split you open from end to end. But then, after that last time, you were the one who held it all in. And that hurts even more, doesn't it? It does, it hurts twice as much when it's not somebody else, when it's you doing yourself in. Because you can do anything, except give yourself space to heal. Because you can do anything, but you can't forget. Because you're the only one you can't seem to forgive: you can't forgive yourself for letting him do it. You can't forgive yourself for being you. You can't forgive yourself for wanting to be someone else. You could scratch your own skin, hurt yourself, set yourself on fire. But you're always going to be stuck inside your own body. So you might as well take off your gloves and step out of the ring.

I bet you could never play a game of hide and seek, let alone make friends with boys. Huh, now that I think about it, I bet you can't fuck either. Because every time a man looks at you, you bow your head. Every time a guy gets near you, it gives you the goose bumps. Every time someone touches your butt or squeezes your tits, you don't want to suck their dick or jerk them off. You must be terrified of touching and being touched. Terrified of them getting near you and their weight pressing into you. I bet you'll never get off again, let alone enjoy a good fuck. You'll be frigid for the rest of your life and you know it. I bet when you look at your friends, those gorgeous sluts, you can't help but wish you were like them. You look at them with their short skirts, with their hair pulled up, shaking their asses, and you can't help but think you'll never be able to do that. You'll never be like them. Because every time you put on a pair of shorts you spend hours in front of the mirror wondering how other guys might look at you. And their desire terrifies you, and those legs that were groped are no longer yours. The legs of a girl, a little bitch of a girl, a neutered bitch.

I don't like the fact that you're with him. He's not man enough for you. Don't you think, Flor? He has no personality. Plus, he's so shy. He wouldn't know how to treat you. If I were you, I'd wait a little longer. You're too young for a boyfriend. I don't like you staying at his house either, spending the night there. I'd rather make sure you're comfortable – here with us. Or don't we take good care of you? I know your aunt doesn't cook, but I always make you breakfast. Serve it to you in bed, nice and hot. Think it over. Who treats you better? You should leave him. Besides, Grandma invites you over every Sunday for a pasta lunch. She even grates the cheese how you like it. And we take you along to San Pedro every time the girls go shopping, to help them pick out their clothes. When did your mum last take you anywhere? You know she always has to work. And in the summer? If it weren't for us you'd be stuck in your apartment in Buenos Aires. But instead you get to come with us to the club, go to the pool all together. I even got you a membership – don't forget you have to renew your card in January. Oh, and the medical certificate! So you can get into the pool with me, we'll play dunking games with Florencia. I remember the first day you arrived. You were covered in lice, like the rest of your cousins. You didn't hear this from me, but after you came to visit we always washed our hair with hydrogen peroxide. And, well, some things never change. But I guess they did fix you up a bit. Helped you lose some weight. You were fat and they took care of you. It didn't take much on our part. Your mum was broke and your dad was never around. They shipped you off wearing nothing but the clothes on your back and a ten-peso note in your pocket. We fed you, you got to eat all your cousin's favourite foods. We spoiled you. On your fifteenth birthday we gave you a sequined t-shirt that you wore with a black skirt. Your back was bare, smooth, tanned by the sun. And your moles – I only get a glimpse of them sometimes, at night. Makes me want to tear them out, one by one, with my teeth. Anyway, it's a pretty t-shirt. That's why I think you'd better stay here. You can't go. Right, Flor?

Listen to me, I have something to tell you. No, I'm not seeing another woman. Nothing like that. Cut the bullshit. This is about your daughter.

Her father wasn't so wrong about Claudio. He had his reasons for not wanting to leave them alone together. No, wait, let me finish. The other day when we were all together eating at your house I noticed something. He doesn't look at her like an uncle should. No! Listen to me! The way he looks at her, it's like he wants something, like he's turned on. Yeah, the way a dirty old man is turned on by a fifteen-year-old girl.

Yes. Really. He spent every minute he could looking at her ass, and I could see him drooling once she'd put on her pyjamas and come down to say goodnight. I could see it in his eyes, and then I knew it was real when he noticed me watching him and avoided my gaze for the rest of the night.

Don't cry. I don't want to upset you, but I had to say something. You'll have to decide for yourself what to do, she's your daughter. It's none of my business. But I'll say it again: it's my duty to tell you what happened. Besides, he fits the bill. He's a psychopath. A textbook case, and you know it. He bought your whole family and he bought you too. He manipulated you. He convinced you of his generosity, and made sure he was beyond reproach. He imposed his authority with everyone's consent. Even his own wife, and his daughter Florencia.

Think about it and then we'll talk.

PROVINCE OF BUENOS AIRES

DEPARTMENT OF JUSTICE
PUBLIC PROSECUTOR'S OFFICE

AFFIDAVIT

Be it known to all persons that in the city of San Pedro, Province of Buenos Aires, a witness has been duly summoned to appear before this prosecutor's office to give testimony. The witness is hereby advised that false testimony is punishable by law and is required to attest and swear to the truth of all matters within their knowledge or as to which they may be interrogated, by pronouncing the words 'I swear'.

When asked about any family or business relationships that may exist between the witness and the parties involved, the witness replied: 'Yes, I was in a relationship with the victim's mother for approximately six years; the relationship has since ended. It is through that relationship that I met her brother-in-law. Notwithstanding the foregoing, I shall speak truthfully in all of my statements.'

Subsequently, pursuant to the provisions of article 101, the witness hereby DECLARES: 'I arrived at my girlfriend's house in Buenos Aires, it was in the afternoon and when I walked in I found him lying down in my girlfriend's bedroom. He had a chronic hip problem and had gone to a doctor's appointment that day and was feeling tired afterwards so he lay down in bed. After I came in the two of us started chatting and we drank a few mates together. Then my girlfriend's daughter got home and walked through the room we were sitting in, and that's when I noticed the way he was looking at her buttocks. Then, addressing me, he made an offensive facial gesture and a comment in poor taste, clearly in reference to his niece's rear end. This took me by surprise and I was speechless because I didn't expect such a comment or that type of gesture coming from him. Despite how uncomfortable I felt after what had occurred, I took a few days to think it over before deciding to mention exactly what had happened to my girlfriend. The reason why I waited so long was because I wasn't sure whether to mention it or not, I wasn't sure how serious it was, and because I didn't want to cause any problems in the family. After I told my girlfriend about it she decided to ask her daughter, and after a short conversation her daughter broke into tears and recounted everything she had gone through as a girl when she went to visit the town of Santa Lucía. She had never mentioned any of it because she was scared about generating conflict in the family.'

'After that I didn't ask any more about it but I felt relieved by the fact that I had mentioned it, because as a result my girlfriend's daughter was able to talk about what she had endured during the summers she spent in Santa Lucía.'

When the witness was asked whether they have any additional information regarding the current investigation, they responded by stating: 'I have nothing else to add.'

The phone rang and I answered it.

'You little whore, what did you say? Tell me it's not true, go on. Tell me that everything your mum said is a lie. How could you do this to us? You killed him. You fucking whore, say something!'

I denied everything and hung up. I denied it like I had been denying it to myself for years. Remembering it every night but forcing myself to believe that I'd made it all up, that it was nothing more than hazy images, that there was no evidence. But this was the first time I had denied it to someone else, and I had denied it to her. How could I do that to her? How could I wreck her family?

Wait. Which family am I talking about? What if he did the same thing to her but she can't bring herself to talk about it? Maybe I'm doing her a favour. But no. He's her dad, he couldn't do that to her. But he did it to me and I'm his niece.

I grabbed my phone.

'I denied it, Mum. I denied it all. How could you tell her? Why didn't you warn me? What am I going to do now? I want to die. Don't you get it? This can't be undone.'

My mum waited for the right time to call him, while his wife was at the gym and Florencia was with her boyfriend. She wanted to tell him that she knew, that it was time for him to stop playing dumb. She thought that he would be able to admit it, but he didn't. Instead he denied it and had a heart attack.

Hello, nice to meet you. My name is Juan. It's a real pleasure to meet you, you're much taller in person. Your mum told me a little bit about what happened. You're really brave, you know that? That son of a bitch is going to jail. How could he go and screw up your life like this? Just look at you, you're a wreck. Don't worry, he's going to pay.

Come here, sit down. Tell me more about it. How did it start? Your mum told me that you were thirteen, but we're better off saying you were eleven. That's how things go with the law. See, you have to exaggerate a little. To all effects, it's the same, right? What difference does it make? One year more, one year less? He raped you either way. Ah, no. That's right, he didn't rape you. Then, why are you here? What was your name? Oh, right. It was *almost* rape. Close, but no cigar. Bloody hell. We would have been better off. This way, our case is screwed. Judges are more sympathetic to rape victims, the younger the better. With just some fingers or groping, I doubt they'll give him more than probation. But, oh well, we'll get something.

Are you sure he didn't penetrate you? Yes, I remember what you told me. If your father hadn't shown up that day then perhaps we'd be having a different conversation. But well, here we are. Like I said in my email, I'm going to need you to be more precise. Date, time, place. Everything needs to be more exact. Yes, I know the images are blurry. It's always the same story. But the judges need facts, not dreams. They aren't convinced by some dumb fantasy. Look, let's try something. Go home, and when you get there sit down and write. Yes, let's do that. Better if you write the affidavit yourself. Take your time to put it into your own words, write down everything that happened to you. And make sure to ask for justice, because nobody else is going to do it for you. Not even me.

That's a lie, there isn't just one guilty party here. I'm not buying that load of bullshit. Listen here, the kid was a minor. There were two adults whose job it was to take care of her, that was *their* responsibility. And you know what? They didn't do it.

This guy waltzed around in his underwear in her house. He took showers with the door open and slept with his shirt off, exposed. He lay down in the same bed as her to take naps, he gave her massages in front of everyone. This guy wanted to pick her up every weekend and take her back to his house. Drive more than two hundred kilometres just to see her. And nobody said a word.

Seriously, listen to me. Didn't they realise it wasn't love? Were they *that* stupid? Sure, her aunt and uncle could help take care of her, but... To leave her there over the holidays, too? On her birthdays? I know, she wanted to be there, she asked to go and she cried every time she had to leave. But, c'mon. Didn't they ever ask themselves why she didn't want to be at her own house?

I opened my eyes. Everything was dark. All I could see was the pale nightstand beside the bed. And feel his fingers inside me, his dick up against my ass. His heavy body was pushing me into the mattress. Again, I couldn't breathe.

I was sleeping on my side, with my head resting on my right arm. When I realised what was happening I tried to force myself back to sleep, but I couldn't.

What would happen if I turned around and looked him in the eye? If I screamed so that everyone could hear me? Or was it better to stay still and let him keep touching me and breaking me. I didn't have anywhere else to sleep.

It was the first time someone had touched me, and it was him. I knew it was him because I could feel his breath, always short and heavy, because I knew his weight, his body. I knew because before turning off the light he had decided to sleep on the floor next to my bed, as if he were doing me a favour, indulging me.

I kept my eyes closed as I felt his thick, hairy fingers groping my vagina. His revolver was on the nightstand. My back hurt. My neck, waist and thighs were getting stiff. I was motionless. Then, without thinking, I jumped up and ran to the bathroom. I didn't turn around because I couldn't bring myself to do it: I didn't have the courage to look him in the eye. I never did. Nor did he, because he always came around at night and from behind. He never looked me in the eye. He couldn't bring himself to see me as the abused or himself as the abuser.

I entered the bathroom. As best I could, I pulled down my underwear and sat on the bidet. It was all stained. A blood clot slipped out. I got a good look at it because it took me a long time to turn on the tap and rinse it down. I was scared that they would hear me and find me there. I was scared that he would open the door or that my aunt would wake up. I had no idea what time it was. Florencia still hadn't come back from the night club.

I sat there, letting a stream of water relieve the pain. I felt a hole in my stomach. I felt like I was on the brink of the abyss. I was terrified of going back and finding him still in my bed. I couldn't, I didn't want it to be true.

The sound of Florencia's keys in the door calmed me down. Surely he wouldn't dare do anything with her at home, but was I ever wrong. I ran back to my room and found him sleeping on the floor, like the night before.

PROVINCE OF BUENOS AIRES

DEPARTMENT OF JUSTICE

San Nicolás, May 2016
Investigative Psychology, Unit No. 5

For the attention of the Public Prosecutor:

As the appointed Psychology Expert Witness
for this case, I herewith inform you that
on 16 May 2016 I conducted an interview with
the victim, as part of my official duties to
provide the required psychological expert
report.

I) PSYCHOLOGICAL ASSESSMENT

a) Diagnostic Material
* Open-ended psychiatric diagnostic interview
* Semi-structured psycho-diagnostic interview
* Bender Gestalt test
* Buck's achromatic house-tree-person test

b) Diagnostic Observations
The Plaintiff demonstrated proper hygiene
and grooming, and was alert and oriented
to time and space. She exhibited a resolute
and lucid demeanour concerning the events
reported, although her composure and tone
of voice became distressed when recalling
said events.

Her speech was clear and coherent, without any contradictions. No fantasy-prone personality type characteristics were observed. However, she displayed indicators of emotional instability, emotional numbness, anguish, fears and difficulties with social interaction, as well as stiffness and eating and sleeping disorders, all of which are consistent with having experienced a traumatic situation.

II) CONCLUSIONS

Based on the examination of the case record, the mental status assessment and the results of the complementary study methods, it is concluded that the Plaintiff displays indicators consistent with having experienced traumatic and sexual situations during her childhood. No signs or symptoms of simulation or fabrication were observed and her account was clear, coherent and without contradictions.

All forms of sexually abusive behaviour towards minors have a detrimental impact on their psychological wellbeing. The severity and expected outcomes of this harm are not necessarily proportional to the type of contact made. The way in which the abuser imposes sexual violence may result in the victim accepting it as normal conduct, thus preventing them from reporting the assault promptly.

In light of the foregoing, it is deemed essential that the young woman continues to receive psychological support with the objective of overcoming these traumatic experiences.

Based on the information provided in this report, it is determined that the Plaintiff is capable of providing a formal statement. This expert report should also be included in the record as supporting evidence.

That's how every summer you handed me over, and that's how they took me in, as a partial payment. I was a package that you delivered in December, after the school year had ended, and picked up in March, all fucked. Virginal upon arrival and defiled upon departure, a voucher that they redeemed a few months later in exchange for presents.

And there you were, impossible to change. Unable to comprehend that the only thing I needed was for you to see me and for you to stay. To not let go of my hand. To teach me some self-respect, to look after me. To search me out upon seeing my empty bed. To pick up my calls and decipher my tears. To get on the first bus and pick me up in the middle of the night, right when he started. To knit me a sweater in winter and sew my murga costume by hand for the Carnival parade. To attend the parents' meetings, the school assemblies. But I also needed you to shoot him dead and take me home with you. Yes, take me home. Look up from your phone and meet my gaze. Be there for me. Don't just hand me off.

Now it's my turn to speak. Listen to me. Do you understand that I'm at my wit's end? I'm destroyed. I lost my whole family. I moved away from my mum, my sisters, the place I was born. I left behind everything I had for you. Even my house, the house I bought before you were born. I left everything, and this is how you pay me back?

Who do you think you are? Do you think you're the only victim here? This happened right in front of my eyes and I didn't realise it. Do you understand the guilt I'm carrying around? I love you so much, I would have given my life for this to have happened to me instead of you, just to be able to save you from some of the suffering. Life is making me pay for it anyway... You were the one to live through it, you were the one who got screwed over, but I carried you in my womb. I gave birth to you, and that's why I suffer through everything that happens to you, but twice as much. Yes, that's right. Everything you felt, multiplied by two. That's how I feel. And you still think that you're the star of this film. It's because you can't stop and take a look around. Don't you see? You might not care, but from now on it's only going to be the four of us at Christmas. Forget about the long tables, the scent of grilled lamb, toasting with cheap bubbly. Now we're on our own, and that's why we have to stick together. That's why you have to stay close. Don't leave! Stay here! Don't you get it? If I can't talk about this with you, who can I even turn to?

You didn't knock out your own teeth. They were knocked out of you, they were yanked out, one by one. You got the shit beaten out of you. You got it good, nice and hard, with clenched fists. And there you lay, spread-eagle on the floor, an open wound. Exposed, dumped on.

No one ever taught you how to drive, you'd never even learned how to change gears. And just like that, no limit in sight, you put the key in the ignition and revved up the engine. You felt like you were flying, you felt free.

When you hit the pavement, broken and bruised, you opened your eyes and found yourself all alone.

I felt like my life was ending on that trip. Hundreds of kilometres in the throes of agony. Never-ending. Who the fuck sent me there to show my face? What a ridiculous idea, thinking I could end all the hypocrisy in a flash. What made me think I should travel three hours to get to town, go from house to house, look them all in the face and tell them, in earnest, that I'd come there to stick my finger up their asses. Strike them with my only weapon, tell them every detail, put them ill at ease. Talk at them for an hour straight, reminding them what his bare dark torso looks like and how uncomfortable it is to wake up with his fingers inside me. Recognise in their faces the signs of contempt and compassion, let them give me a pat on the shoulder. And keep at it, keep talking. Tell them how the man they eat their Sunday lunch with used to fuck me in his own bed while they were out. How he would show up at night while his wife slept, appear behind me with his dick out and rub it against me until he came. Hold their gaze and start to realise how those eyes feigning sadness suddenly had nothing to say. No stopping there – keep them from interrupting me, hurl all the shit right at them. Now it smelled good because it was no longer mine and mine alone. Now every time they see him, every time he turns up at their houses or grabs the hand of one of their daughters, now they'll know what fear feels like. Now they'll have no excuse.

You don't have to explain a single thing to me. I know what you're saying is true. I thought I was going to take this to the grave with me, but I can't stay silent any more.

Once, when I was a girl – I don't think you'd been born yet – I went to pick up Sofia at his house. Yes, our oldest cousin. What happened is that I rang the bell and no one came to the door. Sofia didn't come out. I started to get worried. I rang the bell again, waited a while longer, and just when I was about to leave he opened the door and walked off. He didn't say a word. I walked in and I found her slumped on the armchair with the straps of her tank top hanging down and her eyes filled with tears. When I asked her what had happened she immediately covered my mouth and told me to be quiet. 'This stays between us,' she said.

I always thought it would die with me, but now that I'm hearing this… If she had said something maybe you wouldn't be here now.

PROVINCE OF BUENOS AIRES

DEPARTMENT OF JUSTICE
PUBLIC PROSECUTOR'S OFFICE

AFFIDAVIT

Be it known to all persons that in the city of San Pedro, Province of Buenos Aires, a witness has been duly summoned to appear before this office of prosecution in order to give testimony. The witness is hereby advised that false testimony is punishable by law and is required to attest and swear to the truth of all matters within their knowledge or as to which they may be interrogated, by pronouncing the words 'I swear'.

When asked about any family or business relationships that may exist between the witness and the parties involved, the witness replied: 'Yes, I know her because I'm her cousin and we see each other sporadically. And as for him, he's the husband of my mother's youngest sister. Notwithstanding the foregoing, I shall speak truthfully in all of my statements.'

Subsequently, pursuant to the provisions of article 101, the witness hereby DECLARES: 'I heard about what happened to my cousin directly from her. She called me to see if she could talk to me about what had happened and we agreed to meet at my house in Buenos Aires.'

'After we spoke, not long after, I connected the episodes she recounted to something I'd been told by another one of our cousins around eight or nine years earlier. Her name is Sofía. She's the oldest of all of us. Sofía told me that once he started giving her a massage until, at some point — according to her — she started to feel like the massage was no longer the type that a father would give to his child, nor that an uncle would give to his niece or nephew, that there was nothing pleasant about it and that it was making her feel really uneasy. As a result, she got up from where she'd been sitting and from that day on she could no longer look him in the eye or be alone with him. From that day on everything changed for her.'

'Another time, I was talking with my aunt, and she acknowledged that everything being reported had really happened, saying: "I was so watchful, so vigilant, and yet it happened in my own house." Those were her exact words. After a while, once sides had been taken in the family conflict, Florencia called me and verbally attacked me for not having defended her father.'

'Then I tried contacting Sofía to find out what she thought of all this and once I was able to get in touch with her I reminded her of what she had told me previously and her response was: "To tell you the truth I'm scared. What I told you that day, I'll take it to the grave with me, because this is huge and if my mum finds out she'll go off and kill him, and I don't want to upset her again." Those were her exact words.'

'Nothing like any of this ever happened to me, but I believe her, just like I believed Sofía when she told me.'

When the witness was asked whether they have any additional information regarding the current investigation, they responded by stating: 'He was always really violent. I remember as a girl how worried my mother was, and the rest of my aunts too, because he used to beat his wife, one of my aunts, while she was pregnant with Florencia.'

No one understands you better than I do.

No, nothing.
No, I told you, it's nothing.
Leave me alone.
C'mon, give me a break. Leave me alone.
I can't talk, that's enough. Stop insisting. But *you* can do it. You're young. I've got three kids already.
No, it doesn't matter. I can't. Plus my mum is in bad shape. She couldn't handle any more pain.
No, I don't know what you're talking about.
That's enough already.
Let it go.
It's over.

Yes, dear. Why wouldn't we believe you? You're like a daughter to us. Besides, he always made my skin crawl. You saw what he did to your aunt when she was younger. Nobody has forgotten how he used to beat her up. Don't worry, we're on your side, but with Florencia in the middle it's complicated. She comes over to our house and brings him along, and we can't kick him out. 'If he leaves I'll leave too, and I'll never come back,' that's what she said the last time. I love you and I don't want you to suffer, but Florcita doesn't deserve this either. Poor thing. He's her dad and she's just defending him. Wouldn't you do the same?

Besides, you ran off. You never came back after you told us what had happened. Did you ever think of your grandma? You got upset with her because she still let him come over and visit. She was bedridden, she did what she could. Plus, he lives five blocks away and you, hundreds of kilometres. What could we do?

Don't forget that he took care of your cousins as if they were his own blood, he put them up in his house on weekends. We're all eternally grateful to him. And now we're stuck in the middle. Try to understand where we're coming from, it's not easy. And it's not that we don't believe you or care about you, it's that he chose to stay close and you didn't.

PROVINCE OF BUENOS AIRES

DEPARTMENT OF JUSTICE
PUBLIC PROSECUTOR'S OFFICE

AFFIDAVIT

Be it known to all persons that in the city of San Pedro, Province of Buenos Aires, a witness has been duly summoned to appear before this office of prosecution in order to give testimony. The witness is hereby advised that false testimony is punishable by law and is required to attest and swear to the truth of all matters within their knowledge or as to which they may be interrogated, by pronouncing the words 'I swear'.

When asked about any family or business relationships that may exist between the witness and the parties involved, the witness replied: 'Yes, he's my brother-in-law and she's my niece.'

Subsequently, pursuant to the provisions of article 101, the witness hereby DECLARES: 'I never saw any of what my niece is claiming. I absolutely never saw a thing. Ever since one of my sisters told me that my brother-in-law had abused my niece I couldn't help but deny everything, I didn't believe it. In my mind there was no way it could be true and I didn't ask any further.

'My brother-in-law and his wife (my sister) have always been there to help me raise my daughter Sofía, who lost her father at the age of seven. The alleged victim even asked Sofía to say that she had suffered attempted abuse too. Unbelievable. Sofía got furious when that happened, denying everything.'

'In my opinion, none of this could ever have happened because the girl was always moving around between all of our houses, meaning she spent a little bit of time at each of her aunts' houses. I did notice some peculiarities about her, some of which seemed normal and some didn't. For example, I noticed that as a girl she was always [sic] towards Florencia, and then when she got older she was better at hiding it. In fact, to the point that this lawsuit was filed right when Florencia was going to move in with her aunt, the plaintiff's mother.'

When the witness was asked whether they believe the victim, and if so, then why, they responded by stating: 'I don't believe her. I can't believe her because my brother-in-law raised my daughter and he never laid a finger on her. And also because my niece always said that my brother-in-law and his wife were like parents to her.'

When asked by the public prosecutor what their relationship with the suspect is or was like, they responded by stating: 'I've always had a good relationship with him. He's always been good to us, to all of my sisters, my parents, his nieces and nephews, to everyone, supporting us spiritually and financially when necessary.'

Hi.

Yes. Let's make it quick because I'm at work and I don't want to cry here.

No. Don't call my landline because Florencia is there. Let's talk now. Wait, I'll go into the bathroom.

Tell me. Tell me what happened, when it happened. Tell me the dates, the places. Tell me everything now.

C'mon, speak up. Where did he touch you, where did he hit you. C'mon.

But if he didn't fuck you, then why the hell are you doing this?

This can't be. It can't be true.

Yes, I know. I was there.

Yes. I saw you. I remember.

I know. Enough. Stop talking, please. I don't want to hear another word.

No. I can't leave him. I can't, for Flor's sake. I have to protect her.

No. She can't know the truth.

Not a word out of you.

I don't care.

This ends here.

Don't you ever call me again.

Not you and not your mother.

I'd like to thank you all for coming. I've gathered you all here to tell you what's been going on. I'm sure you've already heard about it from other people. I want to make it clear that my dad didn't do anything. He's innocent, and I can't let his name be dishonoured – not in town and not in the police force. That's why I called you here: for your support, not your judgement. After all, the truth will come out in the end.

Here's what happened: my lease was ending in a month so I figured I'd move into her house to avoid paying a higher rent. I wasn't so thrilled about the idea because I wouldn't even be able to bring a guy home with me, but at least I'd save some cash. Then she had a fit because she assumed that my dad would come to visit once a week. And she couldn't handle it. I always knew that she was a snake, and I've even said so to my parents, but they never listened to me. It's their fault for letting her stay at our house, they should have sent her packing.

Now, this is a little bit embarrassing, but I need to ask for your help. Yes, a contribution, because the little bitch brought charges against him and we can't even afford a lawyer. They told us that he could be dismissed from the force and then he won't even have a paycheque coming in. And we have to keep up on payments for the car, the motorcycles, the house, the apartment and the trips. We can't do it all alone. So, that's why I need your support, the support of his closest friends. Thanks to you he won't go to jail. It's thanks to you that we'll be able to prove that everything she's saying is a lie.

In my opinion, people don't just do what they can, they do what they want. I think my family did the wrong thing in this situation. No. I think they chose to play dumb, they chose to look the other way. They screwed me over. And, you know what else? Acting as if none of this had ever happened is the same thing as backing him up. It's accommodating a beast who was capable of beating the shit out of his wife and fucking his niece. It's indulging a guy who stole their self-worth right out from under them. It's accepting and encouraging the brutalities of a man who thinks he can appropriate a woman's girlhood and destroy it.

Why don't you cover up a little more, dear. Just look at the shorts you're wearing. You're so tall and you have such long legs – it could give men the wrong idea. And you wouldn't want that to happen in *this* neighbourhood. It's not the safest. I'm just looking out for you, like I'd do for my own daughter. I warn her not to dress like that too, especially now that she's started to develop. She'll be able to get whatever she wants now, she just has to show 'em off to the right person. There's nothing wrong with being a little slutty behind closed doors. Anyway, I'm going to wash the dishes before Pablo gets here. Go on out and have a good time. But remember, don't go after some sissy boy. You deserve a real man.

No! Don't tell me to stop! You're a cesspit. All you do is spew shit everywhere. You're rotten. No one loves you. What were you thinking, you little twerp? Who do you think you are to say that about my old man? Open your eyes, you've got nobody. Not then and not now. Everything you say is a lie. Believe me, you're going to have to swallow back every word you spat all over us with that virginal face of yours. I'm going to make you pay for all your bitterness. Because, in the end, you're nothing but a resentful little bitch. Because you want everything that's mine, at any cost, and you don't realise that for that to happen you'd have to be born all over again. But don't worry, I'll help streamline the process for you. I'll make sure you get back all the shit you unloaded on us.

A tight jaw and gritted teeth. The daily grind. Shoulders always tensed up, a crooked spine and a stiff neck that can't turn to look around. And feet, big flat feet that hurt with every step I take. Feet that hesitate and cling to the hard ground, that rub and burn and hurt. Just like every time he hurts me and defeats me by lunging on top of me. Every time I can't breathe, every time I'm smothered by the pressure of his weight on my back and his voice in my head. Every time that he crushes me, that he deprives me of breath. That he deprives me of myself.

You can't just cover the sun with your hand and expect it not to be there. I don't care that you grew up in a bubble, that you've never really experienced pain. I'm not going to take that on. I didn't choose for your dad to fuck me, much less for you to be his daughter, so take your anger out on him, okay? Because he wasn't looking out for you all the times he got turned on by one of your cousins, or when he pushed me against the bed and jerked off while grabbing my ass, and then had the nerve to look you in the face and deny having done it. That's right, Florencia, he was happy to let you keep standing up for him rather than let his pride be wounded.

Please don't die. Seriously, Dad, don't go. Don't leave me alone with Mum. It's just that I can't handle it. You know I can't take it any more. I forgive you, but don't abandon me. I forgive you for everything. I swear. I don't resent you any more. I forgive your absences, I forgive you for becoming a father when you no longer had the energy for it. I forgive you for always having one foot outside our house, for never once saying 'I love you' to me, for forgetting my birthdays every summer. I forgive you for dumping everything on her, for encouraging me to take care of her and not leave her alone, to indulge her any whim, when in truth it was she who should have been taking care of me. I forgive you for not setting limits, for not punishing me every time I mouthed off to you for your lack of courage and your silence, for not speaking out, for not defending me wholeheartedly when I needed it. I forgive you even more for not having the balls to look him in the eye, tell him not to mess with me, that nobody touches your daughter. Yes, you heard me right; nobody fucks her if she doesn't want to. But really, seriously. Really. Don't go yet. Don't leave me alone again.

PROVINCE OF BUENOS AIRES

DEPARTMENT OF JUSTICE
PUBLIC PROSECUTOR'S OFFICE

AFFIDAVIT

Be it known to all persons that in the city of San Pedro, Province of Buenos Aires, a witness has been duly summoned to appear before this office of prosecution in order to give testimony. The witness is hereby advised that false testimony is punishable by law and is required to attest and swear to the truth of all matters within their knowledge or as to which they may be interrogated, by pronouncing the words 'I swear'.

When asked about any family or business relationships that may exist between the witness and the parties involved, the witness replied: 'Yes, I'm the victim's father and I know him because he's the husband of my ex-wife's youngest sister. I lived with my ex-wife for approximately fifteen years.'

Subsequently, pursuant to the provisions of article 101, the witness hereby DECLARES: 'I never liked him from the day I met him and we never got along, but in spite of my feelings we were always on friendly terms because he was the husband of my ex-wife's youngest and favourite sister.'

'Besides the fact that I didn't like him very much, I never would have suspected that he was capable of doing something like this, I never would have imagined it.'

'I remember that he had the habit of showing up at my house in Buenos Aires early in the afternoon on Thursdays and staying with us until Friday mornings, when he left for work. He worked for the police force in the city of La Plata. That is until one Thursday when I got home, around two or three o'clock in the afternoon, and when I opened the door I noticed he was wearing only his underwear, and he walked towards the bathroom, which was next to my daughter's bedroom.'

'I was pretty upset by the fact that he would walk around my house half-naked with my daughter at home. I never said anything to him, but I did talk to my ex-wife to make sure he wouldn't be staying at our house again. After that he stopped staying over. At the time I didn't actually suspect that his behaviour could be related to an attempt at abusing my daughter. He just seemed a little too comfortable making himself at home, along with other habits of his that I didn't agree with, and nothing more.'

When the witness was asked whether they have any additional information regarding the current investigation, they responded by stating: 'I have nothing else to add.'

So your mum abandoned you?

Yes.

Your dad neglected you?

Yes.

Your brother cut off ties with you?

Yes.

Well, it makes sense that you feel angry, but none of them are an accomplice to the crime. The only criminal here is already being put on trial.

I'd better stay here, I don't want to wake up my aunt.

It hurts.

It hurts a lot.

I'm scared of the blood that's dripping, but I can't tell Mum.

The water's helping me feel better.

I got a light-coloured blanket out from the closet.

It's soft.

My feet still stick out from underneath, like always. That's why I'm wearing my light blue socks, even though it's summer.

My aunt woke up to go to the bathroom and noticed me here. She was wearing the same grey nightgown as always.

She didn't say anything.

The futon in the dining room is a little uncomfortable.

After my uncle moved into my bed I decided to come out here.

I hope he doesn't get angry. I only wanted to get a better night's sleep.

My uncle woke me up with breakfast on a white tray.

I was already awake anyway. Flor's not a morning person.

He laughs as he spreads jam on my toast.

It still hurts.

I'm sitting on top of a cushion.

I finished my juice already. It was good. It was fruit punch.

Luckily, it's daylight now.

Night time is still a long way off.

DEPARTMENT OF JUSTICE
PUBLIC PROSECUTOR'S OFFICE

AFFIDAVIT

Be it known to all persons that in the city of San Pedro, Province of Buenos Aires, a witness has been duly summoned to appear before this office of prosecution in order to give testimony. The witness is hereby advised that false testimony is punishable by law and is required to attest and swear to the truth of all matters within their knowledge or as to which they may be interrogated, by pronouncing the words 'I swear'.

When asked about any family or business relationships that may exist between the witness and the parties involved, the witness replied: 'Yes, I know him because he's been married to my younger sister for approximately twenty-eight years and because I am the victim's mother. Notwithstanding the foregoing, I shall speak truthfully in all of my statements.'

Subsequently, pursuant to the provisions of article 101, the witness hereby DECLARES: 'Once, in 2005, I called my daughter's paediatrician and she referred me to a paediatric surgeon who was a specialist in genital problems because of the intense pain my daughter was experiencing in the pelvic region. She claimed that the pain was the result of an accident she'd had involving the seat of her bicycle, which surprised me because of the inconsolable way she cried about it.'

'The specialist we were referred to told me that my daughter had a lesion in the perineal area and asked her whether she'd had sexual relations. She said she hadn't, so it was attributed to developmental changes or the bike accident, and the specialist said that no operation was needed. Neither of the two doctors we visited suspected or mentioned to me at any time anything about a possible situation of abuse. Nor did I suspect that it could have been caused by anything like that.'

'Then my daughter started having problems at high school, she was supposedly very sad there and sometimes they'd even found her crying in the bathroom, so the teachers called us in to discuss the matter together. I feel like she went from being a happy girl to a sad and withdrawn teenager.'

'When I found out, my daughter asked me to keep quiet and not to say anything. This silence lasted until one day when I called my brother-in-law and told him that I knew the truth about everything he had done to my daughter, and that I didn't want him anywhere near her, and that he could say whatever he wanted to his family. He played the victim and denied everything. Then he put down the phone and the line went dead. Right away his daughter, Florencia, called me back saying that we were making things up because we didn't want her to move in with us while she finished up her degree in Buenos Aires. Then my sister called, asking me to tell her the details and everything I knew, but I refused because I was really hurt by it all. So she called up my daughter, and claimed to believe her after hearing what she had to say, but still, she wondered why she hadn't said anything before. She said she wouldn't leave her husband because of Florencia.'

'When my daughter decided to file criminal charges against him, I decided to help her and offer my unconditional support.'

When the witness was asked whether they have any additional information regarding the current investigation, they responded by stating: 'I have nothing else to add.'

Yes, I remember you. You came to see me a long time ago, it's been about ten years, hasn't it? You were young, you must have been fourteen or fifteen. I remember that you lay down over there, on the cot, and that I examined you because you were in a lot of pain. You said that you'd slipped off the seat of your bicycle, onto the cross bar. Isn't that right? You could barely move because you'd landed so hard. Luckily your mum was able to pick you up in town and bring you back to the city right away.

I also remember that I asked your mum to wait outside so that I could examine you and talk with you one-on-one. Oftentimes, I have patients who are scared to admit that they had relations because there's a family member in the room, so I prefer to ask relatives to step outside. I did that with your mum.

When I noticed that you'd experienced vaginal tearing, I thought maybe you'd had your first time, or something else had happened. You said no, that you'd only slipped off your bike seat, and I believed you, but there was still a chance that something else had happened. Besides, you had a huge internal bruise and one labium was bigger than the other. But here we are. If I had known, I wouldn't have hesitated to tell your mother. I believe that everything in life is a lesson. Perhaps now you'll be more careful when you have a daughter someday. And perhaps now I'll be more attentive to my patients.

Hi Mum.

Yeah, I'm good.

Can you come get me this weekend?

No, there's nothing wrong.

No, I didn't have a fight with the girls. Today we're going to the ice cream parlour.

Yeah, it's just that I miss you.

Yes, I want to go home.

Can you guys come? Please.

Well, yeah, that's it. Florencia and I had a fight.

No, nothing serious. Please don't call my aunt. Just come pick me up.

Okay, all right. I'll wait till the weekend.

Yes, I know it won't be long. It's just that sometimes it feels like forever.

I love you. Send my love to Dad and Edu.

PROVINCE OF BUENOS AIRES

DEPARTMENT OF JUSTICE
PUBLIC PROSECUTOR'S OFFICE

AFFIDAVIT

Be it known to all persons that in the city of San Pedro, Province of Buenos Aires, a witness has been duly summoned to appear before this office of prosecution in order to give testimony. The witness is hereby advised that false testimony is punishable by law and is required to attest and swear to the truth of all matters within their knowledge or as to which they may be interrogated, by pronouncing the words 'I swear'.

When asked about any family or business relationships that may exist between the witness and the parties involved, the witness replied: 'Yes, because I was the victim's babysitter and she was under my care from the time she was born until she turned fifteen. And I know him because the victim's mother, my ex-employer, had a sister who he was married to.'

Subsequently, pursuant to the provisions of article 101, the witness hereby DECLARES: 'I started to work as a live-in nanny for the victim's mother in 1998, taking care of the victim's older brother, her mother's first child. Then, when the victim was born, I took care of her until she turned fifteen.

I remember noticing a distinct change in her behaviour when she turned thirteen years old. Suddenly she was always tired, fatigued, or she had a stomach ache, or she was sad, and when I asked her what was wrong she would say "nothing" and, out of ignorance, I attributed it to her transition from primary school to secondary school and to her parents' separation.'

'When she first told me what she had been through, I asked her why she'd never said anything to me and she told me she had been really scared.'

'I remember that even while I was there in her house in Buenos Aires he would walk from the bedroom to the bathroom in his underwear. I also remember how much it upset me that he would leave his gun in plain sight on a shelf in the dining room. That gave me a really poor impression of him, especially since he used to beat up his wife years earlier. And also, now that I remember, every time he travelled to La Plata he would ask if he could take her along with him to Santa Lucía. He would pick her up on his way back since he drove his own car there.'

'She and I still meet up from time to time, but we've never talked about the matter again.'

When the witness was asked whether they have any additional information regarding the current investigation, they responded by stating: 'I have nothing else to add.'

Should we talk for a few minutes so I can tell you how much I regret what you're going through? So I can give you my condolences and tell you how sorry I am for all your suffering? I don't think it would be of much use. That's not what you need. What you need now is to get going. Enough of this, enough beating yourself up. You don't deserve it and those of us who love you don't deserve it either...

I didn't go to my grandma's funeral and I don't feel guilty about it. She had cancer for at least ten years, the morphine stopped taking effect at some point. I hadn't seen her for some time, but I always called her on her birthday and said hello every time my mum passed me the phone. I didn't want to hear her voice, it gave me the goose bumps. I remember that my aunt answered the last time I called, and in a low voice she asked me to wait. 'Grandma will pick up in a minute,' she said, and that was when I heard his laugh. She had let him come to visit her. This house, which had always served as a refuge for me, stopped being mine forever.

She'd been bedridden for years. There was a woman who took care of her and put down a bedpan when she needed to use the bathroom. Other people had to clean up her shit. She never made an effort to use her walker or go out on the pavement to drink mate. She always wanted me to go into her bedroom, where the walls were filled with framed pictures of saints. For me to sit down next to her and listen to her talk. She would tell me stories about the golden years of Perón and Evita, of how poorly she'd felt that week, and of how she hoped God would take care of her and forgive her sins.

The last time I saw her she was crying. She told me that everything would get patched up, that everything was going to get better. I didn't know that the worst year of my life was still to come, but either way I didn't believe her. I was convinced that she just felt sorry for me, because back then I was in such a fine mess not even Saint Expeditus himself could have brought me relief. And she took pity on the defenceless and asked for compassion: she asked the heavens to empathise with me in a way that she would never be able to.

PROVINCE OF BUENOS AIRES

DEPARTMENT OF JUSTICE
PUBLIC PROSECUTOR'S OFFICE

AFFIDAVIT

Be it known to all persons that in the city of San Pedro, Province of Buenos Aires, a witness has been duly summoned to appear before this office of prosecution in order to give testimony. The witness is hereby advised that false testimony is punishable by law and is required to attest and swear to the truth of all matters within their knowledge or as to which they may be interrogated, by pronouncing the words 'I swear'.

When asked about any family or business relationships that may exist between the witness and the parties involved, the witness replied: 'Yes, I know the victim. First because I was a friend of her brother's, and we spent summer vacations together in town, and then because I was her boyfriend from 2008 until the middle of 2015. And I know the suspect because I grew up in town, where he's well-known by everyone. I was even friends with him.'

Subsequently, pursuant to the provisions of article 101, the witness hereby DECLARES: 'When we started to date everything was normal at first. We met in town and we saw each other there. She always stayed at her aunt and uncle's house, until she started staying at my parents' house in 2010, giving me the impression that she didn't want to go back there. That's why I ended up moving to Buenos Aires and started seeing her more often. Eventually, she decided to tell me what had happened. She told me that, many times, when she spent the night at her uncle's house, he had come into the room where she was sleeping and touched her and laid his hands on her. Once he even went so far as to take out his penis and rest it on her lower back. I was the first person she told about any of this.'

'Although she never told me that he penetrated her, everything he did to her had an extremely negative effect on her. She even suffered from nightmares as a result, waking up in the middle of the night almost every night, which is something I witnessed because we lived together for more than a year. All this also prevented her from maintaining a normal sexual relationship with me. Our relationship in general changed for the worse after she decided to talk about what had happened. I think it's the reason why we split up in the middle of 2015, as a result of these episodes that she suffered from.'

When the witness was asked whether they have any additional information regarding the current investigation, they responded by stating: 'I have nothing else to add.'

I can't believe they still doubt your word. They think you'd make something like that up? When sharing what happened degrades you as a woman. They think you'd expose your private life just for the heck of it? Knowing what a mess this has caused in your family! And in town. Not to mention being rejected by men. They'll never see you the same way again, sweetie. Forget it. That's just how it goes.

I can't stop thinking that the two of you split up because of all this. You could have had children together, you were happy. Then you went public and it was all over. Was he ever upset! You know what he's like, he never said a word, but I know this ruined his life. My son loved you and all this has estranged him from his hometown. He can hardly bear to walk down the street anymore. He has to avoid the shops that your uncle frequents. He prefers to drive around in his car, hidden. He doesn't want to come visit as often any more, not even to see his grandparents. He's been on the losing end ever since he took your side. If it had been up to him he never would have stopped visiting us, there's no doubt in my mind. He never would have distanced himself. That's why I go visit him. He needs me now more than ever. And I'll be there, like always, to protect him.

María Elena was waiting for me on the pavement. She was a thin woman around fifty years old. In those days her hair was short and undyed, and that morning she was wearing her glasses. She had just come back from the corner store, stumbling along, weighed down by too many bags. It was the beginning of February, she was sweaty and the asphalt was scorching hot.

The lawsuit had been filed a year and a half earlier. I had written the affidavit myself. I'd already made a statement at three different public prosecutors' offices, and had sworn under oath before a judge who didn't want to ratify my words. And still I'd got no response, not even a restraining order. Meanwhile, not only had he kept his job in the force, but he'd been promoted, and now everyone in La Plata was kissing his ass. I still couldn't sleep at night.

I'd got fed up with people asking me to be patient. Fed up with having to wait. I found out about María Elena one morning when I decided not to listen to my lawyer's advice. I sat down in front of the computer and started my search. For what? Not even I knew. One thing was clear: I needed someone who had gone through the same situation, someone who had been buried in the same shit.

The first time I read about AVIVI, the Association for Victims of Rape, I thought it was a state institution, one of those social centres with secretaries, psychologists and lawyers. More of the same. But no, it was the opposite. AVIVI *was* María Elena: she was its face, she embodied everything it represented. She was the defence in and of itself.

When we met, María Elena grabbed me by the hand and without any questions invited me in to her house in Virreyes. Her daughter Candela lived with her. Candela had been beaten and raped when she was twenty-one years old by a guy who went by the name of Posades and who was known in San Isidro for having attacked another five women, but was still out there on the loose, scot-free. Candela ended up in the ICU for a while, but once she'd recovered it was thanks to her strength that Posades went to jail three years later. This changed both mother and daughter's lives forever. Because from then on María Elena dedicated her entire life to defending her girls. In her eyes, we were all her daughters.

Her office was in the kitchen. She had a white table covered by a chequered tablecloth with five chairs, also white. La Nueva Luna was playing in the background, Candela had tuned in to Radio Delta. María Elena took a pack of cigarettes from her pocket, removed one, and lit it quickly with some matches that were lying on top of the cooker hood. As she did, she also lit one of the gas burners, put on the aluminium kettle for the mate and grabbed a brown paper folder from the filing cabinet where she kept all the documentation. No sooner had she sat down did she start filling in a form with my first and last name and some other personal information, and she asked me to summarise the case in five minutes. When she heard what I had to say she immediately pulled out her two-way radio and said, 'We're leaving. The mate will have to wait.' She knew we had to mobilise, put the lawsuit into action, and there was no time to spare.

'Do you have a car?'

'Yes, my parents are parked on the corner.'

'Okay, then let's go.'

'Where?'

'To the Women and Child Protection Unit. Officer Sosa is expecting us.'

It took us fifteen minutes to get there, my dad really stepped on the gas. When I got out of the car it was me who took her hand. I squeezed it tightly. The queue was endless. There was only one legal expert and, unfortunately, only one Ms Sosa as well.

Hello. Yes, I can hear you.

You called me a little too late, you've already gone and done what you wanted.

I told you to be patient, that the case would move forward in due time.

No, it hasn't been filed away and forgotten, I already told you that.

That lady you found is just looking to stir things up. All that'll do is to piss off the judges when they're just trying to do their job.

I don't care how many years of experience she has, riling them up will get you nowhere.

You have to know how to wait.

I don't understand what's got into you. What are you asking? Whether I've worked on cases of abuse before? No, I haven't. They've always seemed too... I don't know, too disturbing.

What difference does it make? Stop changing the subject.

What's got into you? Are you second-guessing me? Anyway, you've already gone and screwed it up.

Yes, the case has been filed with the province as well. Remember, it was *you* who asked me to file it here in the city, so your uncle wouldn't interfere. Now just look how the tables have turned.

You went behind my back to make one last frantic effort, in the heat of the moment. All for nothing.

Yes, of course I'll get back to you. But I do things at my own pace and sometimes you can get a little worked up. So, calm down and we'll talk soon. Yes. I'll call you in a month.

MOTION FOR CHANGE OF VENUE

Your Honour,

As the lead prosecutor at Office No. 30 for the Preliminary Inquiry of Criminal Cases I respectfully submit this motion for a change of venue for Case No. 74.417/15.

In addition, I hereby request that the proceedings of this case be transferred from the Buenos Aires office to another jurisdiction. Pursuant to article 196 of the National Code of Criminal Procedure (NCCP), I would like to set forth that you may have a lack of jurisdiction in this case based on the arguments presented below.

I. Grounds

Upon careful consideration, I humbly submit that Your Honour may lack jurisdiction at this stage to preside over this case. Therefore, I respectfully request that the proceedings be transferred to the Criminal Court with territorial jurisdiction in the city of Santa Lucía, Province of Buenos Aires.

Whereas events pertaining to a criminal act have transpired across multiple jurisdictions, it is permissible to select only one jurisdiction for trial. In this instance, significant regard must be afforded to the circumstance that the majority of the occurrences associated with this case arose within the confines of Santa Lucía. These events are also the most severe in terms of the associated penalties. Accordingly, it is readily apparent that the incidents having occurred within the aforementioned jurisdiction - totalling nine - may be indicative of a prima facie case for the crime of aggravated sexual assault. This is due to the fact that they were committed with carnal knowledge, and by taking advantage of a dependent situation, as detailed in article 119, third paragraph, section F of the National Code of Criminal Procedure.

It is pertinent to note that the victim's habitual stay at her aunt and uncle's residence, including summers and some long weekends, where she was reliant on their care and support, created a situation of vulnerability that was deliberately exploited by the accused, who engaged in sexual abuse against her, including the act of digitally penetrating her vagina. There is clear evidence that the defendant had carnal knowledge of the minor, as detectable by her vaginal tear in the summer of 2005 (verified by the certificate on file in the Secretary's Office).

In contrast, it is worth noting that only one of the incidents occurred in Buenos Aires. Although the Plaintiff may have perceived this particular episode to be the most severe, considering its unique attributes of transpiring in broad daylight, at her own abode, and while she was conscious, the criminal charges for this act carry a significantly less severe penalty because it qualifies as an offence of simple sexual assault (as per the provisions of the first paragraph of article 119 of the National Code of Criminal Procedure).

In this regard, it is important to bear in mind that acts of sexual abuse typically involve lascivious physical touching of a clearly sexual nature, directed at intimate areas of the body and closely associated with sexual activity. Upon examining the incident that transpired in Buenos Aires through this lens, it becomes evident that it constitutes an offense of simple sexual abuse. This is because the defendant only engaged in physical touching of the victim's back and buttocks, followed by the act of self-pleasuring.

Furthermore, it is crucial that both judicial and procedural efficiency be considered, as well as the need to ensure the seamless progress of the judicial proceedings on behalf of the defendant, who resides in the municipality of Santa Lucía.

II. Petition

Therefore, I hereby request that the Court declare a lack of jurisdiction to adjudicate this case, and therefore transfer the case to the Honourable Judge in Criminal Proceedings with jurisdiction in the municipality of Santa Lucía, Province of Buenos Aires, to rule over the investigation of this case (article 37 NCCP).

Prosecutor's Office No. 30, November 2015

Thanks for calling. I didn't want to bother you until I'd talked to your mum. That way you'd be more relaxed, but I can understand your concern.

I'm holding the dossier in my hands as we speak, right here in San Pedro. It would be good if you could swing by yourself one day so we can look it over together and talk about it. That way I can tell you how things are shaping up for us. His psych report has already been completed, so now only yours is left to do. And the report confirms that he's chargeable, so there are no excuses. He can't plead insanity. Now I just have to compile all the affidavits and the other bits that are missing so we can request that the case be taken to court.

I know you don't want to come here, how hard it must be for you. Your lawyer could make the trip for you, but he hasn't been here yet. Your uncle and his people come to check up on the case regularly. I know it's his turf, but he has every right to do so. It's the law and I have to comply, I'm the prosecutor's right-hand man.

So we'd better move forward. I'm going to call up your therapist right now, and another shrink who sees one of your cousins, one of the ones who lives here. Sofia's already said that she doesn't want to declare. Meanwhile, he's on leave from the force, so he has all the time in the world to think up strategies. Don't be fooled, he didn't get suspended because of you. The police decided not to dismiss him, instead they gave him medical leave for the fourth time this year. I think his last heart attack was just after he talked with you, is that right?

Hey Sis, I'm here with Mum and Dad. I just finished making my statement. I wanted to call and let you know. I hope it helps to calm you down. The social worker wanted to meet us and learn a little more about our family dynamics. She visited town last week, so she's already started to get a picture, but we weren't there for that.

She asked me how you were doing, how all this has been affecting us. I told her you weren't doing so well, nor were we. If everything goes as planned, there are just a few more statements to take down, the indictment, and then we can move onto the oral proceedings. Just think, we're almost there.

It's important for you to take care of yourself. It was a good idea for you not to make the trip this time and to look after yourself instead. Honestly, it's been hard on all of us. She said she thinks it would be good for you to see a psychiatrist so you can start getting a better night's sleep and learn how to navigate your moments of anxiety, like what happened last week. I know you don't want to, and I get that you don't think it's necessary, but it wouldn't be a bad idea to keep it in mind... Perhaps you can bring yourself to do it further down the road, you never know.

Apart from that, she also said for you to call her if anything comes up, that she's here to help. And something else important: she said that going to trial helps women who have been victims to feel vindicated. I know getting this far has already been a victory for you, but just think what a relief it will be if he gets sentenced.

PROVINCE OF BUENOS AIRES

DEPARTMENT OF JUSTICE
PUBLIC PROSECUTOR'S OFFICE

AFFIDAVIT

Be it known to all persons that in the city of San Pedro, Province of Buenos Aires, a witness has been duly summoned to appear before this office of prosecution in order to give testimony. The witness is hereby advised that false testimony is punishable by law and is required to attest and swear to the truth of all matters within their knowledge or as to which they may be interrogated, by pronouncing the words 'I swear'.

When asked about any family or business relationships that may exist between the witness and the parties involved, the witness replied: 'Yes, I know him because he's my mother's sister's husband and I know the victim because I'm her brother. Notwithstanding the foregoing, I shall speak truthfully in all of my statements.'

Subsequently, pursuant to the provisions of article 101, the witness hereby DECLARES: 'As for my sister's allegations, I didn't witness any of them and I never suspected or thought that any of this could happen. I never even imagined it. I found out about it all when my sister told me, in the second half of 2013. She said that she'd been abused by him, but that he'd never penetrated her with his genitals, only with his fingers on some occasions, but there wasn't penetration every time. She always mentioned that he put his fingers inside of her, but she never specified all the details because she burst into tears every time and we always stopped talking about it.'

'She never spoke up because he has an extremely domineering personality and my sister was always scared of him because of the repercussions that her remarks might have in our extended family. She's always seen him as a violent and aggressive person, someone who openly carries his gun wherever he goes. I never saw him like that because he's always been so overprotective of me.'

'I also remember my sister telling me that she thinks our aunt - his wife - may have seen something. One time when our aunt walked by the door of Florencia's room and saw him lying behind my sister, she acted like there was nothing going on, but then my sister heard the two of them arguing about what she thought she'd seen.'

'After everything came out in the open, I tried talking to my aunt, but she sent me a text message that said, "I know that what happened is true, but I can't turn my back on my daughter".'

When the witness was asked whether they have any additional information regarding the current investigation, they responded by stating: 'Yes. My sister was always really fun and carefree until she started high school. It was then that she became sad and was always in a really bad mood. Today, when I think back on it, I realise it coincides with the start of these painful experiences she went through.'

Without any further addition, this document is now concluded as the aforementioned deponent certifies that they have thoroughly reviewed it and have nothing further to add or amend. Therefore, the contents of this document are now ratified, and I affirm that the relevant party appeared before me and subscribed to it accordingly.

You don't understand! Nobody believes her. Our town is so small. My sister and I are the only ones who have the guts to spit in his face. And there's eleven of us cousins! They're all a bunch of fucking wimps! They keep opening their doors to him, they greet him on the street, they still drop their kids off there on weekends. What the hell is wrong with them? Seriously, that man is not to be messed with. He has the police eating out of the palm of his hand and he's one of the owners of the club, the only club we've got around here. Yes, I swear. He decides who does and doesn't get into the pool every summer and he coaches the only football team. I don't know where I'm going to send my son to play when he's older. It may sound like a joke, but I'm not kidding. Oh! And I forgot. Now he's also started to help the priest prepare Sunday mass and he's volunteering with the ladies from Caritas to make sure there's a plate of food for every kid. Do you get the picture? He's ensured himself a reserved seat, front and centre. And he's in charge of the bread and wine in the offertory service. Believe me, that's what it's like. I was never one to take communion, just imagine me now.

Hi there. Yes, I'm Sofia.

Excuse me, but who were you again?

Of course, I understand. Come in.

Yes, I heard.

Look, I don't have much to say.

The truth is that I don't believe what Florencia's saying. It would be impossible for her to go to all this trouble just to kick her cousin out of the house. That's absurd.

But I don't think the whole ordeal is true either, okay?

Just think… Why would she come out with all this now? After so many years?

Seriously, why didn't she say anything before? What do I know, it just seems strange to me.

Well, like I said, I don't have much to tell you.

No, not a word.

I don't have much to say to anyone. Isn't that right, dear?

Let me introduce you to my husband and my twins.

A boy and a girl. I'm very fortunate, can't you see?

Plus, I've got one more who's not here right now, she still hasn't come back from school.

How could I not protect them?

Well, it's time for me to make their afternoon snack.
I think it would be best for you to go.

Yes, of course.
Absolutely. If anything comes to mind, I'll call you.

What floor was it? Do you remember? Let's see, hold my backpack for a second so I can check my phone, I must have it saved there.

I should remember it, we came by here a bunch of times. To think that we received this guy with open arms, just like that little bitch. Look how he's repaying us now.

Ah, here it is. I hope he's here.

Hello, hello? Can you hear me? It's Florencia, from Santa Lucía.

Hi, I can hear you. Are you there? Do you remember me?

Can you come down? I need to tell you something.

Yes, I know you're busy with clients, but well, it's important.

All right, that's okay. No, wait, wait! Don't hang up, listen to me! I'll tell you through the intercom. You'd be better off not even taking the trip to make a statement. Seriously, everything that little bitch is saying is a lie. You'll regret it, mark my words! My dad is incapable of doing anything like that and you, as a professional, should know.

No, wait, listen to me! He didn't come here himself because he prefers not to speak up. He keeps a low profile, but I'm not going to let things end up like this.

Seriously, stop! Listen to me for a second!

What? What do you mean you saw him? What did you see?

Tell me, c'mon. Answer me, you son of a bitch!

Come down! C'mon, come down and say it to my face.

Come and say it to me. C'mon!

All right, go ahead.

Go on and do whatever the fuck you want.

That fucking bastard can go to hell.

Why is he defending her now? He's not even with her mum any more.

Who does he think he is?

All right, that's that. Let's keep going. That other lady's place is just a few blocks away.

Are you coming with me?

Yes, I'm up to speed on the case. I know what they're saying about Sofia, but I don't know if it's true. What do I know? She denies it. And that's fair enough, everyone says what they want and what's best for them, right? Everyone around here is self-centred, everyone wants her to speak up so the guy will go to jail, but then they couldn't give two shits about what happens to her. What's she going to do to provide for her children? Without his help she can't even put food on the table.

It's the same thing they did to me. They got all worked up because I kept going over to his house, to visit Florencia. And well, yes, he's there too, but, what do I know. I can't avoid it. Besides, what good does it do to judge him? We've all made mistakes.

I know you asked me to come here today because of what they said about me. My cousins should all just zip it. But the true is I have no reason to lie. It was nothing bad. He came into my room once, I had my back turned and he unfastened my bra. I got scared because he caught me off guard, but he only wanted to give me a massage. I was all stiff so I let him. At no point did things get out of control, I don't know why they're exaggerating. Most likely the same thing happened with her, but she's just blowing it out of proportion. And here we are, divided.

Is that enough for today?

You always sought out vulnerable girls. Someone said to me once: 'there's no such thing as a single victim'. And they were right. I don't know how many more of us you fucked, I'm sure there were a lot, I know of at least one. And, believe me, you're a textbook case. You eased your way into our family, with a gun in your hand, and fished out two likely specimens. Young girls with absent fathers, with mothers who took refuge in alcohol or depression. Either way. You pried your way in with your thick dirty fingers until you found the right profiles to match your perversion. And then you got what you wanted: to touch us and fuck us however you wanted. And even better, you managed to keep us quiet. That's what turned you on the most, what truly fascinated you. Keeping silent was always the worst punishment for the other girls, and for me too. Speaking out is such a release, but they still haven't broken free from their chains. Not even after looking me in the eye. I saw them and I saw myself. They're still in your hands, under your power, and your strength paralyses them. They take shelter in the love you give them, in the certainty that you are family, in the warmth of your embrace. But they don't see – they can't see – that behind all that everything collapses and they can only fall into the void. Back to where they started, but without the pain between their legs.

Hi there, listen up. I've got news.

By now it seems like everyone in town has heard about the criminal charges you filed and they're starting to call up the firm.

Yes, you heard me right. Two women have called already.

No, I can't tell you. Their identity is anonymous.

Try to understand, it's to protect the case. Don't get upset.

Anyway, listen to this, they both said they'd been victims of abuse by him. One of them he beat up and the other one he screwed.

I mean, yes, he raped her.

By force, of course.

You know what I mean. Don't make me nervous.

What I meant to say is that now we have other female victims and that's important. Now we'll just have to wait and see if they want to come in and make a statement.

The problem is that they're both from town and they're scared.

They said exactly the same thing: 'Don't let anyone find out'.

So we have to be really cautious. This stays between you and me.

I'll call you when there's news.

Hello. Good morning. Am I speaking with Ferrari, the solicitors?

Ah, perfect. Could I speak with Juan?

Yes, of course I'll hold.

Hello, Juan. Sorry to bother you.

My name is Isabel, I'm from the Achaval ranch, right outside of Santa Lucía. Do you know where it is?

I'm calling because I heard about the case against the police commissioner and I wanted to help.

No, nothing happened to me, but something did happen to one of the women who works for me and, well, also to my partner.

No, he's a man. But he's in the force, too, and he knows him.

What happened to her is complicated.

She agreed to me calling you but I still don't know if she'll want to make a statement.

A few years back she used to work at his house. She cleaned there once a week, every Wednesday. Then, from one day to the next, she quit and came here to work with me. She never wanted to talk about it until we heard that they'd opened up a case against him. She says that twice, after his wife left for work, the guy threw himself on top of her and tried to grope her.

Yes, right there in his house, while his daughter was sleeping. The first time she thought it had been a misunderstanding, so she stopped him and kept cleaning. The second time, she pitched the broom and took off.

No, with Roberto it was different.

One evening he was on his way over to my house, dressed in civilian clothes, and the guy stopped him and asked for a bribe because he was driving without his lights on.

Roberto didn't want to pay and then the guy smashed one of the windows on his truck.

He also threatened to throw him off the force.

Luckily nothing happened and he kept his job.

This guy is trouble. Seriously.

It's not that easy. Neither of them want to have problems with him. She's even more reluctant. She's scared. Roberto can get another job, he can leave the precinct and that'll be that. But her, what will happen if he gets a hold of her at night?

Living in fear isn't an option.

But well, what do I know. I'll keep you posted.

Yes, I'll tell them to call you.

No, I can't promise you anything.

Good morning. My name is Juan.
Isabel gave me your number.
Yes, that's me, the lawyer. How are you?

Sorry to bother you, but I wanted to know if you've thought any further about making a statement.

Sure, I understand. All right, it's okay if you don't want to.
Yes, seriously, I understand.
Not even anonymously? You don't know how much it would help the case.

Just think, if you speak up he could go to jail. Or would you rather have him free?
Nothing's going to happen to you, I can get a restraining order so he won't be able to get near you.

What? What do you mean he lives two blocks away?
Oh, I didn't know that.

Well, but seriously, we can protect you.
No, it's not a no-man's land. Now that she spoke up everything has changed.

Okay, all right. If you change your mind you've got my number.

No, don't worry. I'm not here to judge you.

Calling them victims is like screwing them all over again. And again. It's convincing them that their lives have been fucked up for good, that their story starts and ends right then and there, with the guy still inside them. It makes them believe that he created them, that their identity has been constructed from the rape, that their rights were violated and now nobody can guarantee they won't get fucked all over again. They become convinced they have to hide themselves away and keep their legs shut, that it's their fault and they deserve this as punishment. Yes. Because first and foremost they're *his* victims, but they're also victims of themselves: once he came inside of them they were willing to give up anything else they might still have left, even their own life. Yes, you heard me. So hike up your skirt and get ready, because the next step is to bleed it all out. But from the inside.

Hey there! Come on in, sit down. I was just preparing a snack for the two of you. Flor's getting changed, she just got back from the doctor. How was it at the swimming pool? Did you go with the girls? Good thing you got a chance to cool off, it was so hot today. I went to pick up your aunt from the bank, and on the way there I was thinking, how's about we do something in the backyard for your birthday? Your mum told me she couldn't come because she has to work, but I could cook up a little barbecue and ask your aunt to make a chocolate cake. With jam in the middle, just how you like it. We'll buy some Fernet and that's that. C'mon, you're sixteen now. Invite your girlfriends to come over and Flor will call up some boys and we'll be good to go. Don't worry about it, it's no trouble. We'll do it this Saturday, what do you think? And on Friday, when your aunt gets off work, you can go into San Pedro and buy something pretty, dress up a little. What do you say? I'd say to go for one of those short skirts with little ruffles and bright colours like you wear in summer. Ah! But no high heels, you're already too tall as it is. Besides, it would be hard to walk in the grass, in the yard. And we'll have to see if it dries out after that storm we had yesterday. Okay, then. It's all set. There's no need to say thank you, you're like a daughter to me, I've already told you that.

He touches you at night and in the morning he smiles at you, treats you like a queen. He says nice things about you to his friends, praising your height and your curves, and then goes off for the wank of his life in the bathroom. He calls you niece, says he loves you like a daughter, but he desires you and wants to fuck you as hard as his obese body will let him, without a condom, like he does to his wife. He sees you walk by in pyjamas and his dick gets hard, as hard as the baton he uses to beat the shit out of the boys locked in their cells. He takes you with him everywhere, shows you off like a diamond in the rough, but behind closed doors he screws you, splits you open and crushes you, he devours you like a hunk of meat that he's been roasting in his backyard for years. He calls you up on the phone, takes care of you when you get back from a night out at the club, gives you advice and reconciles you with your mum every time there's a fight. He defends you against your cousins, celebrates your birthdays, gives you the best presents, makes you feel loved. But he also touches you, hurts you, rams his fingers inside you until you bleed. He treats you like an object, like a piece of filth for him to eat all day and shit out at night. Because that's what he does to you: he turns you into excrement, into food mashed up by his disgusting intestines and expelled by his dirty ass. He makes you feel like the worst squalor. He convinces you that it's your fault, that you deserve what he's doing because you're a slut. He convinces you that you have to pay your dues for the right to sleep in his house, to feel loved. Loved by him and by any other man. That's right, because he does love you and take care of you. But don't forget: first he fucks you and shits all over you.

Come in, come in. Sit down over here. I'm so sorry I had to ask you to make the trip, but we needed to do this. I knew you'd rather come with a friend and not your mum or your dad. Any problems? This will be the last interview, then you'll be able to rest up and they'll be the ones who have to talk. So, try to relax.

All right, I'm going to ask you to copy these drawings. Yes, take a look at them and redraw them as closely as possible. In the meantime, I'll just keep talking so you don't get bored.

I have to say, you're just how I pictured. It's obvious that you live in the city, but you can't shake your accent. You drop your esses like we do and you love drinking mate. Can I serve you another? I've heard all about you. First the public prosecutor and then your family, when I went to Santa Lucía. I can't say much about them, they certainly have kind words for you, but it doesn't do much good in practice. Oh, here's a pencil sharpener if you need one. He drew them really well. His psych report came back positive so he's in his right mind, there's no doubt about that. As I was saying, I spoke with your parents and your brother, too. You're lucky, not everyone would stick their nose out for someone like that. Not everyone has people who believe them, especially if it's been several years. Let me tell you, rape cases are two a penny around here. Luckily, I'll never be out of a job. But the work really wears you out: talking with all the men, shaking their hand. It makes me sick.

Oh, you've finished already? That was fast! What a shame, this chat has been so interesting. Well, yes, that's it.

Let me give you my card. Give me a call, any time of day, no need to feel ashamed. After all, you've got to let it out, every last bit. But all of it, eh?

PROVINCE OF BUENOS AIRES

DEPARTMENT OF JUSTICE
PUBLIC PROSECUTOR'S OFFICE

AFFIDAVIT

Be it known to all persons that in the city of San Pedro, Province of Buenos Aires, a witness has been duly summoned to appear before this office of prosecution in order to give testimony. The witness is hereby advised that false testimony is punishable by law and is required to attest and swear to the truth of all matters within their knowledge or as to which they may be interrogated, by pronouncing the words 'I swear'.

When asked about any family or business relationships that may exist between the witness and the parties involved, the witness replied: 'No.'

Subsequently, pursuant to the provisions of article 101, the witness hereby DECLARES: 'I began to see the victim in May 2011. She requested treatment to better manage family issues and to address a certain degree of anxiety she was feeling with regard to her brother's upcoming change of residence.'

'During her first year of treatment she mentioned an episode related to her mother's health, saying there were fights and yelling with her mother. She also spoke about situations in which her mother became demanding.

And she discussed her relationship with her brother, and how she felt very protected by him.'

'In our second year of treatment, she started to delve into the details of her frequent trips to Santa Lucía. She talked about feeling protected at her aunt's house after the fights with her mother. She maintained a close relationship with her aunt but, paradoxically, her aunt, uncle and Florencia simultaneously criticised her, expressing that she did everything wrong. She didn't have her own space to sleep in and they made her clean the house, damaged her personal belongings, excluded her, and treated her differently from their daughter Florencia. The victim also mentioned that she didn't feel like she belonged to either of the two families.'

'She also referred to feeling objectified, due to the innumerable favours that her aunt received from her mother, and because the housing provided by her aunt and uncle served as compensation for those favours.'

'At the end of 2012, she told me that years earlier her uncle had sometimes slept with her, which she mentioned as the reason why she no longer wanted to go to her aunt and uncle's house in Santa Lucía. This struck me as relevant but I decided not to press her about it and just wait until she was ready to tell me the particulars of the situation.'

'It wasn't until 2013 that she told me about an unfortunate episode she'd experienced at her mother's apartment in Buenos Aires, during which she mentioned having been abused by her uncle again, without reaching the point of penetration. Her father's arrival at the apartment forced her uncle to stop.'

'When the victim came to my office she seemed very solemn and serious given her young age. She kept her emotions contained when expressing herself and seemed quite self-critical with regard to essential daily activities. Gradually, she started expressing her emotions more, and once she had filed criminal charges against her uncle for the abuse she really opened up.'

'Before she filed the charges, she was scared to tell her family about the incidents she had experienced. Her greatest fear was how it might affect her aunt or her father, who already had health problems.'

'I noticed that having to talk about her uncle's abuse at the courthouse always had an extremely high emotional cost for her. She repeatedly expressed her fear of him due to the fact that he was a member of the armed forces — the police. Every time there's been activity in the case I've noticed an increase in her levels of distress.'

'By being able to voice her situation, she has learned different and better ways of relating with others. Nevertheless, I still consider that the whole situation has had a very high emotional toll on her.'

When the witness was asked whether they have any additional information regarding the current investigation, they responded

by stating: 'I have nothing else to add.'
Let it be stated for the record that a copy
of this affidavit has been provided.

Without any further addition, this document
is now concluded as the aforementioned
deponent certifies that they have thoroughly
reviewed it and have nothing further to add
or amend. Therefore, the contents of this
document are now ratified, and I affirm that
the relevant party appeared before me and
subscribed to it accordingly.

Every time I think that it's over, that once and for all I've finally said everything I have to say, it somehow comes back to haunt me. It comes back in every voice that sounds like his, in every photograph from my childhood, the memories with my family, the town where I took my first steps. It comes back every time I get on a bicycle or the swings at a park, when summer comes and I miss the window displays at my aunt's shop. But it also comes back in nightmares, in scratches on my body, even in the pain of other women's stories that I hear and who share the same emptiness. It comes back every time I see a gun on TV, when I catch some guy looking at my ass, or when people ask me if I'm feeling better.

And every time I relive it I feel the same way: this will never end. And I fight with myself to destroy every image, to try and curb that pain that surfaces every morning and rips my guts out. I blame him for being a real son of a bitch. I blame my aunt for turning a blind eye. I blame my parents for their absence, my paediatrician for not noticing my battered vagina, and also my lawyer for being a soulless jerk. But it's never enough.

Can you talk? Yes, let me tell you how it went. I just got done. I was in there for three hours. I said everything I had to say. I remembered almost everything, everything we've talked about these last few years. At one point I mixed up the dates, but the public prosecutor was quick to help me out. He asked why I believed you and I told him that when I first found out what had happened, I called up your aunt and she told me that it was all a lie. That he'd had a heart attack because of some problems at work and there were no criminal charges. She said that it was just a town rumour. I told him that she lied to me from day one and that you didn't, you were sincere. I also decided it was important to tell the prosecutor how he used to beat up your aunt while she was pregnant with Florencia, something she's sure to deny. But well, it's her word against ours, isn't it? Now whatever happens is out of our hands. I was the last one to make a statement, you asked more than ten of us to go in and we all did it. It's time for the indictment and for him to present his defence. You know I'll be here for you no matter what, all the way to the oral proceedings. I've got your back. Rest up.

Start to let it sink in that it's really over. You have to come to terms with it; there's no need to suffer any more.

I'd never heard you get angry and it makes sense that you're furious, it was time. But now it's time to give yourself some closure and start to tell yourself another story. The story of your life, which doesn't end here. This is just the beginning.

Three years had passed since the last time I went. I didn't think about it, I got a message and decided to go back. I asked my brother to drive, it took us two hours to get there. The town welcome sign, the car zig-zagging between potholes, the cows blurring in with the trees and the scent of feedlot. All this was part of the folklore, and it felt good.

My grandmother's bed was empty, she had died three months earlier and I'd decided not to go to say my farewells. 'I'm not up to putting on appearances,' I thought. But the truth is that sometimes I missed her. My relationship with her had been unusual. I never got to taste her food, nor was I interested in learning much about her life. She was always in bed. That's where I met her and that's where she died. The walls of her room were covered in holy cards and in mildew, and she always cried when she spoke of the past and when she bid me farewell, asking the Holy Father to protect me. 'Take care of yourself, dear, because danger is always where you least expect it,' and she was right. The only thing I remember, because of her insistence, is how much she loved Perón, and Evita too. She always wore her hair in a bun to look like Evita. Not that it matters. Going back to her house to find her room empty was hard. The bottle of rubbing alcohol and her sky-blue handkerchief remained untouched on the bedside table, and the wooden cross on her headboard seemed bigger than ever. A shiver ran down my spine. I don't know if I really wanted to go back. The empty chicken coops were still there in her yard and a flower had finally bloomed, right next to the tomb of the twins who had died at birth. The paint on the walls outside was still peeling, and lone bricks were strewn about here and there.

Scaling the walls with my cousins and running along the roof was, for the other girls and I, the most fun every summer. To say nothing of the treehouse and riding one of our cousin's horses. He taught us how to ride them before we could even walk. We got over our fear quickly.

When I arrived at my cousin's house she was there waiting, glad to see me. She was one of the few cousins with whom I had decided to keep in touch. She was so surprised to see me, she was ecstatic. It was her only son's first birthday, a little prince who was always smiling. I held him in my arms all afternoon. I took care of him so I didn't have to take care of myself. It was tolerable. There were people who I didn't want to see, aunts and cousins who I didn't want to greet, but it was actually quite simple. I just sat there and held onto him. Then, from one moment to the next, I grabbed my car keys and left.

I had forgotten about the dusty streets. The roundabouts and all the unmarked speedbumps. Osvaldo Soriano's voice on the radio, the train station, the San Martín theatre and Pepe's kiosk, where I used to drink ice-cold Cokes after I got out of the swimming pool at the club. How nice it feels to dodge the kids riding their bikes down the street, throwing water balloons at their neighbours. The peace and quiet at siesta, when everything is shut and even the babies sleep. And the exquisite smell of freshly rained on soil after a storm.

When I opened the door to her house I got goose bumps. How noble of it to wait for me like that, austere, humble. The green of the patio, the impatiens by the gate, the tall, tall walls… It was all still there. When I walked in I felt that it… that she… embraced me and closed the doors. I had left thinking that it wasn't part of me. And now I'd returned, empowered, to reclaim it. 'Don't worry princess, time passes but fondness remains.'

Good morning, how are you? I'm Ricardo, from San Pedro. I wanted to get in touch with you directly, like you had asked, to avoid intermediaries.

Exactly. Your case was filed with the local court as well. It's a question of jurisprudence, I'm sure your lawyer has explained it to you. Right. Most of the events occurred here, so taking it forward corresponds to our prosecutor. Yes, even though the last time – the most serious instance in our opinion – happened there, at your house in Buenos Aires.

Like I told you before, I don't want to force you to talk about it all over again. I know you've already spoken to the authorities and you've recounted the same thing a thousand times. So, I carefully read over your case and I'm only going to ask you to answer a few more questions. Yes, the last ones. Just some details. It would be really helpful to be able to add them in. If you're ready, I'll start.

Do you think that your uncle also abused his own daughter?

Giving them a name doesn't stop them from screwing you. Calling them abusers is doing them a favour. It's reducing their madness, their perversion, to a minor display of negligence. It's letting psychopaths get away with a reasonable label – men who don't just force a girl to fuck or use their fingers to rob her virginity until she bleeds. No, they also beat her up and bang her until she's nothing but dust.

Was he violent with you at any time? I mean, that is, aside from these events.

Love me or I won't love you. Love me or I won't let you be loved. Because, trust me, there's nothing easy about loving you. And I was there when you were born, I saw you grow up among us. I even saw you play and flirt and tease. But you weren't like the rest, believe it or not. Your tantrums were louder and there was no way to keep you satisfied. Only your mum could do it, but when she wasn't there I had to take charge. Your aunt already had her hands full with Florencia. And I never wanted to close the door on you. As you grew up, I knew that taking care of you was like betting on the future. And I also knew, believe you me, that I would be the only winner. All girls need a male role model and I wanted to be yours. But I also wanted to make sure that you didn't forget me. I wanted you to cry on my shoulder. I wanted to hold you in my arms. I wanted to open up the world to you, give you your first fuck, help you learn that love should always be part of it. Yes, it was love. Believe me, I didn't want you to suffer. I only wanted to prepare you. It's just that – don't you see? That's how I was taught. And I wanted to share it with you, don't blame me. I wanted to open doors for you. I wanted to help you join the ranks. I wanted to arm you with emptiness so that you never had to feel that pain again. That first time, when you bled – go on, just try to tell me that it didn't turn you into a warrior. The rest. I admit. Was an excess.

How do you explain the absence of your parents?

Hi Uncle, I need you. Mum isn't doing well again, she went back to the doctor and I don't want to stay here. Yes, she's been yelling at me and slamming doors. I'm scared. She's calmed down a bit now, they gave her something to take and put her to bed. She's sleeping. No, Dad isn't here, he couldn't come. Any chance you can start out now? My brother's going to a friend's house, I don't want to stay here this weekend. I want to go to your house. Okay, all right. I'll be here waiting for you. Can you leave work early? That way, if you want, you can pick me up when I get out of school and we can go straight back. I'll pack a bag. Maybe Flor wants to come along, too. We could make a road trip out of it. Thanks. Thanks for coming to get me. I love you, Uncle.

In your affidavit, you say that these acts happened between eight and ten times. Could you be a little more specific?

I don't know how or when, but I was able to let go. Let go of everything that had felt like an immense wave in a stormy sea, sucking me in but never returning me to shore. There was no shore. It took my body, spun it in circles, tore it to pieces. There was no stopping it. I couldn't say no. Let alone all the times when I didn't see the wave coming. When danger, or rather abuse, was my sole reality. Only when I realised that it would cost me my life was I able to let go. And here's the reason why: everything I'd lost became my shield.

Why do you think it bothers you when people look at you from behind?

On my bed, naked, all fucked. Here I am. My legs spread wide open on the bedspread all soaked in cum. He couldn't hold it in, all it took was the slightest graze against my silk sheets. The room is still dark but there's even more darkness in my chest. Because when he's inside me it hurts, my skin splits from the force of his fingers. But once he gets up, once he leaves me there like a used body, like a cunt all stretched out and penetrated, the pain is worse. Because he leaves, but I know he's going to come back. Because as he draws away, the void inside me grows and there's nothing to relieve the pain. I'm haunted by this emptiness every time he pulls up his trousers and opens the door to leave. And it *is* emptiness, because as I watch him finish off and walk away, part of me leaves with him and I become the remains. Because with just one thrust he breaks me and takes what he needs, what he desires, whatever he wants from me. And the leftovers stay there, spreadeagled, the useless refuse to be disposed of. The scraps. My scraps. My body.

What type of consequences did this have for you? If there's more than one, I'd appreciate if you could list them for me.

Whores fuck better because they fuck without fear. I fuck with shame, with pain. And it hurts because I don't get wet, because when someone touches me I don't get turned on. Because hearing the voice of a man whispering into my ear doesn't affect me in the least. I'm excited by their looks, I'm excited by their hands, but I can't bear their touch. Just imagining them brush up against me makes my skin feel like sandpaper and my hair stand on end, my tits too. I enjoy when they close their eyes, when I can feel them come inside me. But I can't stop from hearing, my eyes can't rest, I can't stop my sphincter muscles from tightening up. I haven't been able to experience much pleasure in life, and this you can tell. It's clear in my gaze, it's clear in the way I walk, it's clear in my voice. Who am I fooling? I feel guilty. Guilty for waking up and not being the victim everyone expects me to be. Guilty for choosing to fuck after I've been fucked. Guilty for wanting to get wet, for desiring lots of men, for wanting to climax every day, for smiling at them instead of feeling contempt. Guilty for wanting the pain to end. For wanting to end the pain. For wanting the end. Of this.

Are you tired of people asking you questions? Get used to it, because you're not out of the woods yet. They ask you why you kept going back, why you didn't say anything, why you let yourself get fucked. Forget it, they're never going to approve of what you say. They're always going to question you. You and your word. Putting a man under a microscope always has a price, sweetheart. His manhood, his machismo – they carry more weight than your integrity and the integrity of the other girls. Have no doubt about this. But don't go feeling special. It happens to all the girls. To the ones who file charges and the ones who don't, to those who keep their secret locked away and those who shout it to the four winds. And God forbid you should call into question someone who carries a gun. His pistol carries more weight than his dick, not to mention that he's a believer. And those who do vouch for you will be few and far between, while those who look the other way will abound. It's always easier to turn a deaf ear than to tackle something head on, to take responsibility. It's always easier to drop your trousers and fuck a girl by force than to keep them on and ask permission. So don't get upset, because his manhood crumbles every time you sit your ass down and write. Tear him apart with words, finish him off with a full stop and fuck him between commas. Without further ado. No more shame, no more pain, no more giving yourself over.

Give up the long skirts and trousers and start to show off your legs. Get rid of the loose blouses and shabby old shoes. Don't worry about using high heels, if a man can't get it up because of how tall you are, that's his problem. Don't take it on. Cut your hair, shave it on one side, dye it any colour you want. Fuck a guy or a girl, or both, whatever you like more, just do whatever the fuck you want. Yes, what *you* want. Not what your mum wanted to be and couldn't, not what your dad hopes for before he dies. Don't be the trash that son of a bitch thought you were.

DEPARTMENT OF JUSTICE

San Nicolás, September 2016
Investigative Psychology, Unit No. 5

For the attention of the Public Prosecutor:

San Pedro
Hand-delivered

The Medical Expert Witness and Psychology
Expert Witness humbly address this Honourable
Court and respectfully state:
   That the suspect underwent medical and
psychological examinations on 14 September
2016 to conduct the expert witness reports
as required.

PSYCHOLOGICAL — PSYCHIATRIC EXPERT WITNESS REPORT

I) RECITALS

a)   Personal Information
Age: 50 years old
Address: Santa Lucía, district of San Pedro
Occupation: Police commissioner, retired
Marital status: Married

b)   Personal History
The Defendant asserts that he is a
native of the city of San Nicolás, albeit

subsequently having relocated to Santa Lucía with his mother, who began working as a cook at a ranch.

The Defendant reports having experienced the typical illnesses during primary school and adolescence. At the age of thirty-nine, he underwent hip replacement surgery and was fitted with two titanium prostheses. Earlier this year, he suffered a myocardial infarction, requiring the placement of five stents, which resulted in his early retirement from the police force. Prior to that, he held the position of police superintendent, forming part of the bomb squad, in the city of La Plata.

With regard to his sentimental attachments, the Defendant married in 1988 and from this union his daughter Florencia was born, currently aged twenty-seven and residing in the city of Buenos Aires. He maintains a good relationship with his wife and denies any history of intimate partner violence.

The Defendant asserts his life was comparatively peaceful and comfortable until he was informed by his sister-in-law of the criminal charges filed against him, which coincided with a heart attack on the same day.

Habits: the Defendant does not smoke or consume alcohol. He reports no history of addictive behaviours.

He has no history of psychiatric or psychological treatment.

II) PSYCHOLOGICAL — PSYCHIATRIC EXAM

a) Diagnostic Material
* Open-ended psychiatric diagnostic interview
* Semi-structured psycho-diagnostic interview
* Bender Gestalt test
* Draw-a-person-in-the-rain test
* Pigem's question

b) Personality
The person under examination is a male possessing an age-appropriate physique who demonstrates proper hygiene and grooming. However, his demeanour is defensive and determined by a certain degree of emotional lability, evidenced by a tendency to cry. He expresses ideas of prejudice and defence-lessness in relation to the allegations brought forth in this case.

His behaviour and personality demonstrate alertness and orientation to time and space. He exhibits a dysthymic mood, focused on displeasure and distress.

During the interview, the course and content of the Defendant's thoughts did not reveal any psychopathology.

He displays indicators of low frustration tolerance and a tendency to respond with poor impulse control. His affect is blunted.

Additionally, he shows signs of empathy deficit disorder and a lack of critical thinking. He has a limited capacity for introspection regarding his actions.

Structurally, he has an integrated personality and is suitably adjusted to reality and situational awareness.

His thought content and process are appropriate for his degree of education and sociocultural level.

His memory, attention and will are intact.

III) CONCLUSIONS

Based on the case record proceedings, the examination performed and the results of the diagnostic study methods, these Expert Witnesses consider the Defendant's mental status to be within the parameters of normalcy.

At the time of examination the Defendant has the capacity to understand the criminality of his acts and to manage his actions. No signs of irrational behaviour are noted that would make him a danger to himself or others.

This Expert Witness Report shall be included in the record.

So, tell me, what does it feel like to be abused?

TRANSLATOR'S NOTE

This book begins with an accusation: why did you come back every summer? The speaker's voice is colloquial and familiar, intimate but scathing.

As readers, we experience some sixty fragments that reveal the conflict little by little, always through the eyes of a family member or professional (legal counsel, pediatrician, therapist) involved in the case, as well as multiple layers of the author's voice, Belén, 'talking back': whether it's her younger, more vulnerable self at the time the abuse happened, or her strong present-day self who bolsters that girl she once was. These fierce viewpoints are interspersed with legal statements from her parents and cousins, as well as expert witness reports on the psychological condition of the victim and her abuser. The cumbersome legalese in these real affidavits is in a different font, formatted to look as if written on a typewriter. The plethora of voices and the fact that none are named, as well as their shift in registers, add to the complexities of the book, making it a real challenge to translate.

Readers must assemble the puzzle of who is speaking through hints that are often subtle and apparent only through the character's register or word choice. Each voice has a unique tone and there are over twenty speakers in this slim book, meaning this collage of styles reads, at points, like a set of monologues or even a play. As the translator, it was vital for me to maintain the orality of each entry so the reader could determine which character was speaking.

In the English translation, each account is followed by a blank page. The editors at Charco Press and I decided to insert these pauses to give readers some space to breathe before the next voice began. I imagine the whole book as a theatrical work, where each voice speaks with brutal honesty, showing their true colours. The blank pages serve as 'blackouts' between each voice on stage.

After completing my initial translation, I read the book out loud, imagining each character's voice. Choosing which terms of endearment or insults the characters used were a real source of deliberation for me: calling someone an 'imbécil' ('moron', 'asshole' or 'twerp') or 'puta' ('bitch', 'slut' or 'whore') can be interpreted quite differently depending on who the speaker is and what their relationship is like with the person they are addressing. I was able to consult the author about who some of the unnamed voices were supposed to be, asking their general age and background, to help make more specific decisions about which types of expression they might use. I was nervous to approach the author with my questions, perhaps because of how personal the book is. I wanted to gain her confidence, and not come off as a novice. I didn't have any trouble analyzing sentence structures, understanding slang or cultural references in this book, as I sometimes do when translating other authors. Every author I've asked questions to when translating their work has been different in terms of their receptivity and involvement in my translation process. Belén was warm, professional and succinct in her answers. What more could a translator ask for?

Aside from the oral, colloquial fragments, another challenge was re-creating the book's overly verbose Argentine Spanish legalese. These heavy, tedious texts are interspersed throughout the book, alternating with the mélange of familiar voices. As a reader, this created a sense of exasperating ineptness in me, reminding me of my inability, as a layperson, to penetrate the complexity of the legal system without legal counsel. I felt it was essential for me to consult lawyers here and abroad to better understand these convoluted documents. According to Belén, the affidavits and expert witness reports are the actual legal documents; they were not written specifically to form part of this novel. I wanted their density to come through in my translation, while also making them accessible enough so that readers wouldn't skip them entirely, since they are an indispensable part of this story. I discussed these and other translation problems with many friends, one of whom said that they felt a translator's work resembles that of a 'paisajista de contextos' (a landscaper of contexts). And so, when I went back to editing my translation, I tried to imagine myself as a landscape gardener: hard at work, snipping away to form a hedge, a solid block to give my readers a ground to stand on. Or framing a scene with geometric plants to create all the layers embedded in the text by the author. When I saw my friend again, I asked them to elaborate on the metaphor and it turned out they had been referring to a different meaning of 'paisajista', meaning a landscape painter and their job of recreating a scene as realistically as possible, but, for example, having to work with an entirely different palette of colours just as a translator must make use of a different set of words. The painter forges ahead, with broad brushstrokes, fully aware they are creating something new but that will always be compared to the original scene. Bold yet flawed is the landscape translator: even my original understanding of the concept 'paisajista de contextos' was mistaken! Only by questioning my every interpretation as a translator can I be assured I have begun to glimpse an author's true meaning. It is a humbling profession, indeed.

Being able to discuss the essence of a word or concept's true meaning in another language, and then proceeding to articulate this other culture in one's mother tongue, is also quite rewarding. I have lived in Argentina for thirteen years, and have begun to blend in with the local landscape. This means it is important for me to try and introduce readers to Argentine culture, while also leaving certain untranslatable words in Spanish. If readers have never heard of 'mate' or 'dulce de leche' or 'alfajores', I try to add context around the term, quietly, and without betraying an author's style. For example, when Belén's narrator addresses her mother saying that all she needed was 'for you to […] sew my murga costume by hand' I slipped in 'for the Carnival parade' at the end of the sentence to help readers understand this particular landscape: I hope they will at least sense that a murga is a local festivity involving costumes and a parade, drumming and dancing.

I want readers of my translations to encounter the sounds and smells and tastes of things they don't usually come into contact with in their own culture. I want them to try and understand the underlying currents of a different society. For example, based on whether someone takes part in a murga, an Argentine might be clued into which socio-economic class this character belongs to, regardless of where they live in this vast country. And merely mentioning a murga will invoke, for locals, a very specific drum beat echoing out on the streets in the summer heat of February. During the cymbal breaks, colorful youth dressed in flashy satin clown-like costumes with sequins and funny patches strut back and forth, then squat and suddenly rise in a trio of kicks I can only describe as akin to the moves of a break-dancer kung-fu fighting, or rather, a seven year-old break-dancer practicing their karate kicks in a floppy hat.

Meanwhile, a murga in Argentina is entirely different from a murga in Uruguay, where choral groups of men sing political parodies also dressed in flashy costumes, but wearing clown make-up. In both countries, the murga dates back to the colonial era and involves a parody on the typical role-reversal between master and slave found in many cultures that celebrate Carnival, but here the performance is purely street drumming put on by youth groups formed at neighborhood associations. It can be hard to find anyone participating who is over the age of eighteen.

There just isn't room in Belén's book for me to add all this back story. Plus, being such a culturally-specific phenomenon, my personal description of what a murga invokes (self-expression, freedom, and community), surely differs from what a local or other foreigner will tell you. My own views and experience inevitably seep into my work, and yet I must try to be neutral. In this regard, I feel the translator's job involves subtlety. Like a landscape gardener or artist, I must choose what to highlight: which shapes are the most important to outline, which combination of colours must be obeyed to maintain the book's inner landscape, its soul.

Lopez Peiró wrote this novel before the verdict to her lawsuit was resolved. In January 2023, nine years after she originally filed her complaint, her uncle was finally found guilty and sentenced to ten years in prison. She wrote a piece for the Spanish newspaper *El País* that was published on the day of his sentencing, expressing her relief at finally being able to name him:

> It's over. That's it. It's finished. *C'est fini.* I'm free. What more? After nine years and a criminal complaint. Affidavits, expert witness reports, trips back and forth to police stations, district attorneys, national courts. A five-hundred page case record. Two lawyers. One prosecutor. A justice commission. Fifteen years of therapy. Half my life! My entire family split in two. A whole town covering up the abuser. Seven years of writing workshops. Two books published. Finally. Finally… Now I can say out loud all the names I once could not.

Helping to bring Belén's story to a wider audience has been such an honour. I'd like to thank her for opening up to me and discussing all the events – painful and traumatic, but so important to name and to get right. She answered my many queries about her complex family tree and the sequence of events in this book. I only hope to have done justice to her vision when reworking her words into English. I'm also grateful to the editors at Charco Press for reading several drafts of my translation and helping me to find the weak spots, and for having the vision to publish Belén's brave account. I've learned so much from this entire experience.

Maureen Shaughnessy,
Bariloche, Patagonia
September 2023

CHARCO PRESS

Director & Editor: Carolina Orloff
Director: Samuel McDowell

www.charcopress.com

Why Did You Come Back Every Summer was published on
80gsm Munken Premium Cream paper.

The text was designed using Bembo 11.5 and ITC Galliard.

Printed in November 2023 by TJ Books
Padstow, Cornwall, PL28 8RW using responsibly
sourced paper and environmentally-friendly adhesive.